CH
UP
BUTTERCUP

THE LILLYMOUTH MYSTERIES

BOOK THREE

R. A. Hutchins

The characters, locations and events portrayed in this story are wholly the product of the author's imagination. Any similarity to any persons, whether living or dead, is purely coincidental.

Cover Design by Thia Whitten at PixelSquirrel

ISBN: 9798862161021

To Happy Endings
May We All Find Them

Other Murder Mystery Titles by this Author:

Baker's Rise Mysteries -

Here Today, Scone Tomorrow

Pie Comes Before A Fall

Absence Makes the Heart Grow Fondant

Muffin Ventured, Muffin Gained

Out with the Old, In with the Choux

All's Fair in Loaf and War

A Walk In the Parkin

The Jam Before the Storm

Things Cannoli Get Better

A Stitch In Key Lime

CAST OF CHARACTERS

BISHOP BOB ALTHORP – Daisy's boss

ARCHIE – Mynah bird

CATHY BARNES – Local baker

STAN BARNES – Local baker

DAISY BLOOM – Parish vicar

WENDY BLOOM (DECEASED) – Daisy's grandmother

COUNCILLOR BARRY BRIDGES – Local councillor

MARTHA BRIDGES – Wife of local councillor, on parish council

ROBERT BRIGGS SENIOR – Local landowner of Briggs' Farm

CHARLIE BUCKLEY – Maggie's son.

MAGGIE BUCKLEY – Sylvia's friend, works at Tourist Information office.

GERALD BUNCH / MARCUS CALDWELL – Local florist

RON CARMICHAEL (DECEASED) – Sylvia's husband

SYLVIA CARMICHAEL – Wendy Bloom's best friend, Vicarage Housekeeper

DETECTIVE INSPECTOR RHYS CLUERO – Local detective

GEMMA DALTON (NEE SANDERSON) – Co-owner of local pub, the Crow's Nest Inn

PAUL DALTON – Gemma's husband, works at Briggs' Farm

ANDREW FREEMAN – Bea's husband, joiner

BEA (ABIGAIL) FREEMAN – Owner of Bea's Book Nook

DAISY MAE FREEMAN – Daughter of Bea and Andrew

PERCY GLENDINNING – Local bank manager

VIOLET GLENDINNING – Wife of Percy, head of parish council

DANIEL HARPER – Bea's dad

MORAG HARPER – Bea's mum

JACOB – Vicarage cat

BUGSY MALONE – Sylvia's house rabbit

DETECTIVE INSPECTOR MICHELLE MATLOCK – Local detective

DETECTIVE CHIEF INSPECTOR RICHARD ORNSLEY – Chief detective, Whitby headquarters.

JOE (JOSEPH) PIERCE – Café owner at 'The Boatyard'

BILLY SANDERSON – Co-owns the Crow's Nest Inn with his daughter Gemma.

JOHN SMITH – New Curate

MILDRED SPRATT – Church organist

LYDIA STANLEY – Works in planning department at local council offices

TERRY STEWART – Local Policeman

ROSEMARY WESSEX – Local librarian

CONTENTS

1. AN ALMOST PAINFUL INTRUSION

Daisy let out a sigh of contentment as she put her feet up on the sofa at the vicarage, the warmth of the summer evening wafting in through the open sitting room window. Calm and quiet prevailed for once, mainly due to the fact that her housekeeper, Sylvia, was on a retreat in Scarbrough with her book club ladies. No crazy cop shows on the television, no tense animosity between the vicarage cat, Jacob, and Sylvia's house rabbit, Malone, who had been reluctantly placed in his carrier to accompany the housekeeper to the cottage by the sea.

Bliss.

Daisy reminisced happily on the day she had just spent

at the train station for the opening of the new summer attraction – a steam engine ride. The summer weather had decided to bless the town for once and the sun had shone down in all its glory, leaving the vicar with a small amount of sunburn on the back of her neck. Still, nothing could dampen her happiness. Her erstwhile best friend Bea had been more like her old self than Daisy had seen her all year, even asking if the vicar would like to hold little Daisy Mae while she served customers at the refreshment kiosk. Her husband, Andrew, basked in the praise he received for having brought the old station rooms back to their former glory and Daisy had high hopes that her tentative friendship with the couple would soon be back to its previous closeness.

Then there was Bunch. The town florist, Gerald Bunch, had kept his promise of being a friend to Daisy, nothing less and nothing more, and they had had a lovely day with the villagers used to seeing them out and about together now. Did Daisy still have feelings for him that went beyond friendship? Yes. Was she going to admit that to the man himself? Certainly not. In fact, Daisy's attraction towards the florist grew weekly, to the point where she now had to mentally stop herself from reaching out to touch his face or grab his hand, but the vicar had no intention of pursuing her errant emotions. No, everything was going well, so why rock the boat? Given the lingering looks that he regularly sent her way, Daisy was pretty sure the growing attraction was mutual, but she respected the fact that Bunch kept his promise and never alluded to the emotions bubbling under the surface of their relationship.

Even Daisy's adversaries in the town – namely Robert Briggs and Violet Glendinning – appeared to have paused their respective campaigns to have Daisy removed as parish incumbent. That, along with the news that the Bishop was finally appointing a curate to the parish to work alongside her – a nice man who had popped round to the vicarage to introduce himself last week before he started in a fortnight – meant that Daisy's chest was for once free of the heaviness of responsibility that she so often carried.

As always, there was just one black cloud on the horizon. The one that never left and wouldn't do so until Daisy uncovered a killer – her Gran's murder. No further forward on that front than she had been when she returned to her childhood home of Lillymouth, Daisy had wondered more than once whether she should try to let the search go. Whether she would in fact be much happier if she tried to draw a line under the horrific and tragic incident which had shaped so much of her life. On the one hand, what a lightness of spirit, what a de-burdening Daisy knew she would feel if she allowed herself to walk away from the trauma which plagued her nights and weighed down her days. On the other, what guilt would she feel, what failure even, if she never found the justice she sought for Gran? It was a conundrum which Daisy could never untangle herself from.

She refused to think on it now though, when the day had been close to perfect, when evening's balmy warmth was washing over her to the extent that Daisy didn't even feel like she needed the pain relief that her body normally demanded at this time of day. No stresses, no distractions. No polite conversation to be made or parish duties to be fulfilled. They were all tomorrow's problem and Daisy wallowed in the feeling of contentment that had eluded her since her return to the town.

The sound of hammering on the vicarage door was therefore an almost painful intrusion into the vicar's quiet musings. Daisy wondered if she could avoid answering – if she hunkered down quietly and pretended no one was home she could perhaps get away with remaining in her contented bubble for a bit longer. No such luck, however, as Archie the mynah bird swooped into the hallway from the kitchen giving his best rendition of a doorbell and in doing so unsettling Jacob who had been dozing peacefully on Daisy's feet. Where moments before there had been silence, there was now a cacophony of animal noises to add to the din of the hammering which, Daisy noted, had only increased in intensity.

"I'm coming, I'm coming," the vicar tried to speak above the racket, "don't get your knickers in a twist!"

All humour disappeared from her voice, however, when Daisy was met with a white-faced, apparently seriously stricken young lad, whose hand shook as he pointed in the direction of Church Street, "Out there, Vicar, someone needs your help!"

Daisy didn't recall seeing the boy before either in church or around the town. He looked to be no more than fourteen or so, all skinny limbs which he didn't seem to have grown into yet.

"Oh! Is it one of your friends? Have they had an accident? Fall off a bike?" Daisy tried to get more details as she turned away to get her shoes out of the cupboard under the stairs. This was what she was here for, she supposed, to serve her parishioners as best she could, whether they were young or old.

When no answer came, Daisy pivoted on one foot, one shoe on and the other dangling off her hand, only to find the teenager gone. No sign of him on the path through the vicarage garden or on the church driveway as she peered out of the open door either.

Must've cycled back to his friend to say help was coming, Daisy assumed, grabbing her walking stick from the coat stand and hurrying after him as fast as her unhappy hip and leg would allow.

2. DÉJÀ-VU OF THE WORST KIND

Now, if Daisy had been more astute or less trusting, she might have wondered why the lad didn't use his mobile phone to call for medical help. After all, no teenager is without one nowadays, are they? Or perhaps to call a parent. None of this crossed her mind, however, as she happily left the sanctuary of the vicarage with neither handbag nor her own phone, simply grabbing the door key and warning her adopted pets that they'd better have calmed down by the time she returned.

Daisy exited the church grounds through the thick, wrought-iron gates that were never closed and turned right onto Church Street, which she assumed was the direction of the boy's vague hand gesture. Still no sight of the teenager himself, however, nor of anyone in distress. Nothing to set Daisy's alarm bells ringing, either, as she made her way towards her own car which was parked on this side halfway up the road. Would it be better to park it on the church driveway? Probably, but the crime rate for car theft was so low in Lillymouth, and the hassle of reversing out onto the street every morning not at all appealing, hence the vicar left her little runaround on this adjacent street.

If the vicar had not been so recently basking in the stupor of a day well spent, she might have had her wits about her before she tripped over the body and managed to get blood all over her shoes. Equally, she may well have thought twice before she picked up the knife that lay protruding out from under the rear bumper of her car. Perhaps she would have realised that the young lad didn't have a friend in need – after all, he'd never actually said as such – and that he had been hired simply to give her a message, hence his disappearing act. Unfortunately, none of this struck the vicar until after the fact, when her hand held the bloodied murder weapon, dripping onto her summer dress, and her mind registered the glassy eyes of none other than Detective Michelle Matlock.

"Oh my goodness!" The vicar shrieked, dropping the

large knife and staggering backwards. Were it not for her walking cane, she would have stumbled into the church wall. As it was, Daisy stood hunched over the aid, her breaths coming in shallow gasps as the familiar tightening took hold of her chest and her head swam with dizzy nausea.

The sirens barely broke through the vicar's consciousness, not even when two police cars parked up alongside her, swiftly followed by an ambulance. Daisy's head was thick with the fog of her panic attack, so she didn't register until much later that someone must've called the emergency services, must've arranged for them to be there at the exact moment of her grisly discovery.

As it was, everything passed in a blur, the handcuffs attached to her wrists, being led to a police car by a detective she had never met before, the wait in the hot, stuffy vehicle while the officers performed their ritual investigations around the body. The metallic tang of blood filling Daisy's nostrils, combined with the sharp smell of vomit, though she had no recollection of having been sick. The yellow stains on her dress told another story, however, mixing with the red in an unholy pattern.

It was déjà-vu of the worst kind, as Daisy recalled

finding her grandmother's body all those years ago. Seeking an apparently safe space in her mangled psyche, her mind latched onto the florist's shop. Happy childhood memories. Relaxed evenings shared more recently with Gerald. The smell of lilies… Daisy wasn't even aware she had fainted until she was rudely and aggressively shaken awake by yet another hitherto unknown detective, this one full of questions to which the vicar had no answers. By this point, she could barely recall what had brought her outside in the first place, let alone why she was currently locked up in a police car. Shock had descended on Daisy like a heavy shroud and she didn't seem to have the energy to fight her way out of it. There was no friendly face to latch onto, no kind word of reassurance to soothe her, so Daisy allowed herself to drown in the cloying thickness that filled her mind and paralysed her body.

"Reverend Bloom, come on now, Vicar Daisy, it's me, Detective Cluero," the gentle lilt of the Welshman brought Daisy back from her inner musings long enough to recognise that they were outside the main police headquarters in Whitby. Apparently the small station in Lillymouth had been shunned in favour of the larger, seemingly more official building into which Cluero now gently led the shaking vicar.

Daisy had no idea what time it was, whether the lovely day at the train launch had been today, or even simply a figment of her imagination. The vicar's hold on reality seemed to have slipped in the same way it had in the days after her grandmother's murder. The years between having melted away to leave the husk of a frightened teenager in a woman's body.

At least Cluero was a familiar face, and Daisy knew instinctively that she trusted this man, as she allowed herself to be led through numerous sets of alarmed double doors to a small room deep in the bowels of the building. The vicar sat where the detective indicated, noticing then that they had at some point on the walk here been joined by one of the aggressive investigators from the murder scene. Instinctively, Daisy felt for her dog collar, that symbol of reassurance that she was no longer a frightened juvenile, and was under the Lord's care. Finding it missing, as she had been wearing a sundress for the day's festivities, the vicar felt bereft – almost naked, in fact – and hunched over the black metal table, her head in her hands.

Momentarily, a white plastic cup filled with water appeared in the vicar's line of sight. "Have a drink, Reverend Bloom, I've asked them to make you a sweet cup of tea for the shock, but we need to ask you some questions first," Cluero's tone was soft and Daisy took the cup in her hands but simply held it there, not lifting it to her mouth.

"Right then," the other officer, whom Daisy was to learn was Detective Chief Inspector Richard Ornsley, was obviously keen to get down to business, if his brusque tone and pinched features were anything to go by. A man of short, wide stature and decidedly sweaty appearance, he had a world-weary air that had evidently seen too much to ever be shocked again. Certainly, with Daisy, he gave off the blasé confidence of having the murderer right there in front of him, thankfully no detective work to be done, and he sighed loudly before pressing the relevant buttons as if this were simply a tedious formality to be checked off his list. The recording machine was started, the legalities of names and rights taken care of, and then the questions began.

The interminable questions, which made Daisy's head swim faster than it had before.

How long had she been planning to end the life of her former high school bully? After all, she must've harboured the hatred for many years, letting it grow and fester. Was that her real reason for returning to Lillymouth?

Why had she sent a text message to Detective Matlock

asking her to meet on Church Street and intimating a crime had been committed? Was it to lure the policewoman to her death?

Was the knife from the vicarage or had she purchased it new?

Did she have a doorbell camera to prove someone came asking for help or equally to prove what time she left the vicarage?

"We don't even have a working doorbell, it's broken like a lot of things around there," Daisy whispered, "and I told you I've misplaced my phone. I just bought a cheap one last weekend until the original turns up. You can see on the parish Facebook page I informed everyone of my temporary number."

"Hmm, do you have a receipt for this purchase?" the unrelenting Ornsley asked.

"I suppose so, it was from Argos," Daisy rubbed her temples, willing the pounding inside to stop.

"Perhaps a break would be…" Cluero began asking his superior, just as a uniformed officer knocked and poked their head around the door. As Ornsley left the room to speak to the man, Cluero paused the tape and whispered, "Daisy, this is not looking good, not good at all, you need to think lass. Think hard now. Everything is at stake."

They both looked up as the Chief Inspector returned, assuming his seat and crossing one ankle over the other knee languidly, "So, Reverend Bloom, a witness has come forward who saw your violent act, committed before the sun had even set and in such a public place. You couldn't possibly have hoped to get away with it, could you? Committing cold blooded murder in plain sight. Read her her rights, Cluero, I'm positive the Crown Prosecution Service will sign off the arrest, even so early in proceedings, given all the evidence. It's an open and shut case."

"What? No! I didn't kill anyone!" Daisy heard her shrieked cry, felt the sobs as they wracked her body, was aware of Cluero formally arresting her as if through a wall of cushions, detached as she was from the horror of it all.

All the vicar could do was pray. For this to be one of her awful nightmares. For God to intervene and stop the whole thing.

For peace.

3. A VICAR IN NEED OF SHELTER

Daisy awoke in her own bed for the first time in days and for once was comforted to feel the heavy weight of the vicarage cat on her feet. Jacob seemed to sense her delicate mood, and for once chose not to take advantage of it, instead keeping a close guard on Daisy all night from the bottom of the bed.

It hadn't all been a nightmare, of course, for Daisy had spent the last days locked up in Whitby, attending first the Magistrates' Court and then the Crown Court to request bail. It had been touch and go whether or not she would be granted this, with the police arguing the added doubt cast upon the vicar over her grandmother's death some fifteen years previously should be reason enough to think she might act again.

Her own solicitor, a friend from her past life in Leeds who Daisy had used her one phone call to contact, had counter argued that Daisy was in no way a threat to anyone in the community, and that her exemplary record as a vicar and previously as a victim liaison officer should be taken into account. In the end, bail had been granted, hence Daisy being allowed to come back to the vicarage to await her trial, which would not be for several months.

The vicar knew she should feel a sense of relief that she was not still banged up. That she had time to make a case and present her innocence. Maybe even to find the real killer. But in truth Daisy was exhausted. And scared. No fuel in the tank and no inclination to find any. She wanted to hibernate here, with her Bible and her cat, and never speak to anyone again. The vicar hadn't yet heard from the bishop, but no doubt her job would be in jeopardy owing to her currently being a criminal, and so her home in the vicarage too. Especially as the new curate she'd had tea with in the vicarage was already lined up.

Daisy couldn't give that any headspace. Shepherding a flock may be her vocation, but right now the vicar herself was in need of shelter. So, she snuggled back down, startled awake from her dozing by a knock on the front door. Even just that seemingly normal sound filled the vicar with panic, to the extent that she had to slowly and deliberately calm her own breathing as she prayed Archie wouldn't cause a noisy scene in the hallway. Thankfully the pets had had plenty of food and water in the boot room and so had hardly seemed to notice her absence.

"Daisy! Daisy!" Bunch's voice drifted through the old stone walls of the cottage.

Of course, the vicar's arrest would be front page news in the quiet town. Even without Sylvia to keep her updated, Daisy knew she would be the main topic of conversation the length of Cobble Wynd and in all the local social media groups. And yet she couldn't bring herself to care. Daisy knew her own innocence and that was enough. A small twinge of guilt that Gerald and Joe would have found out on the grapevine rather than from her directly had been quickly smothered in the million and one other thoughts Daisy had had in that bare cell and she had even less inclination to deal with the man face to face now.

"Daisy, love, please, Cathy Barnes said she saw you being dropped off in a taxi last night. Why didn't you call me?"

As much as she didn't want to face her friend, nor did Daisy want his side of the conversation to be conducted so publicly, being shouted through the vicarage letterbox, so she hauled herself to her feet, fought off the dizziness which came from having eaten very little, and stumbled along the hallway to the front door.

"Gerald, come in if you mus…" Before Daisy could finish her sentence she was enveloped in a huge bear hug.

This was the last thing she needed, as no doubt it would set the waterworks off again and she wasn't sure she had any tears left to shed, yet Daisy couldn't help but lean into the man, welcoming his familiarity and warmth, the faint smell of fresh greenery always embedded in his waistcoat. A safe harbour in a storm, to be sure, and for a brief second the vicar wondered why she hadn't asked Cluero to call her friend in the first place. But then, she'd hardly been thinking clearly.

"You've lost weight, and you're as white as a sheet, love," Bunch held her at arm's length for a moment, frowned deeply and then hugged Daisy to him, even tighter this time. As if reassuring himself she was alive and breathing. Again, she couldn't bring herself to protest. "I'll put the kettle on and make you some breakfast, shall I?"

"I don't think there's much food in. No milk either,"

Daisy whispered.

"No worry, I'll call and ask for some to be delivered. I know the locals are keen to help..."

"No, Gerald. Goodness no! Thank you, but I don't need any help," Daisy spoke as firmly as she could with the little energy she had, "in fact, I was just going back to bed."

The much taller man looked down at her for a moment, the deliberation clear across his features, before he startled Daisy by sweeping her into his arms and carrying her to the bedroom.

"Gerald, what are you..."

"Doing? I'm getting you back to bed. Then, if it's okay, I'm going to hold you in my arms for a while, just to prove to my desperate heart that you're here and safe, before I go out and buy food and begin looking after you. Then, I'm not going to stop looking after you. Okay?"

"I, ah, well, I'm not sure that's," Daisy's voice was muffled against his neck as Bunch carried her back to her bed and then laid her down as if she were made of precious glass. Dispatching the offended feline off to the armchair, he tucked the blankets around her gently before lying down on top of them and extending his arm in invitation for Daisy to snuggle closer.

A moment's hesitation was all it took before the vicar was welded to the man's side. Her traitorous body desperate for his solid reassurance and her mind in need of feeling safe just long enough to get a decent hour's rest. His long fingers stroked through her wild hair, his voice soft with words of calm compassion as his heart beat a comforting rhythm under her hand. Yes, Daisy just needed some help to get enough sleep to clear her head. Without medication which would cause the mental fog to build and not dissipate.

Then she would be independent again.

Daisy was sure of it.

4. ONE OF THE GOOD'UNS

The hot summer weather had finally been replaced by a few days of torrential rain, which was much more common for north Yorkshire whatever the season. Daisy was glad of it. The cool breeze through the bedroom window, the rhythmic drumming of the raindrops against the glass, it soothed her so much more than the sticky, sweaty heat of the past week.

Gerald hadn't been able to stay long in the vicarage, despite dosing up on antihistamines for his animal allergy, and so swiftly moved Daisy into his spare room above the florist's shop. For the vicar, it was almost as if she had come full circle, and that in itself was a bit disconcerting. Bunch assured her he could take care of her better if she were closer and could more easily fend off the queries of the local community for Daisy if she remained here with him. Since Sylvia was back to look after the vicarage menagerie and Bunch had fitted a new camera doorbell and deadlock for the housekeeper's added safety, Daisy had agreed it was the sensible option. She had to admit to feeling more removed from town life, from the chance of gossiping tongues and whispered accusations up here in her childhood bedroom and that alone helped her heart to settle. Combined with Gerald's attentive care, which never crossed into ungentlemanly territory, Daisy was beginning to feel safe again.

Of course, for the unmarried vicar to move in with the man who had made monthly public proposals since her arrival was shocking to some of her parishioners, but Daisy could honestly say that this was low on a long list of worries. After all, what could be worse than having your parish incumbent charged with murder? Of course, the vicar couldn't hide away forever, and today they were due a visit from the bishop himself. At any other time, a face to face home visit would be considered favouritism indeed, but in this instance Daisy was pretty sure he just wanted to let her go gently. To give her her marching orders in a more 'Christian' way than by letter or over the phone, since so far Bunch had done a good job of fielding all calls so that Daisy hadn't actually spoken to her boss since the arrest. Gerald had cited Daisy's strained mental health and physical incapacities, her desire to get things straight in her head before discussing any big changes and so on. No doubt this had left the prominent clergyman little choice but to arrange an in-person meeting.

Naturally, the head of the Church of England in the diocese couldn't be visiting one of his employed flock in the small flat above a florist shop, so Daisy had to decamp back to the vicarage for the morning.

"So good to see you, petal," Sylvia enveloped her in a warm hug, "though you've lost weight, I can tell just by looking at you, you need some of my homecooked meals in you lass." The last was spoken with a pointed look at Bunch, who was currently sneezing into a large cotton handkerchief. Daisy was well aware that Sylvia didn't approve of the vicar moving out of the vicarage, let alone to the florist shop, as she had chewed Bunch's ear off about it at least three times that week already via text message. No doubt frustrated that the man in question declined to answer her calls. The florist may have gradually ceased performing his act over the past few months, let his façade fall almost completely the majority of the time, but the townsfolk still treated him like a buffoon. Daisy wondered if they were even aware of his softer, more intelligent tone or whether people simply heard what they wanted to.

"Gerald has been feeding me very well," Daisy replied, feeling like an animal in the zoo.

The housekeeper merely tutted and lifted a tea towel that had been resting over a plate on the kitchen table, uncovering a homemade carrot cake with a flourish. Daisy knew she should be grateful, and did try to demonstrate that sentiment, though inside the nausea grew so strong that she had to turn away from the sweet offering. Being back in the vicarage was harder than she had imagined. The memories of that evening, the reality of her whole situation hitting her again with the force of a freight train. Other than a strong desire to take refuge in the church, to pray and to seek guidance, Daisy would've happily never left the safety of the florist's again. Not at all realistic, she knew, but her anxiety didn't care for the truth right now, much preferring to live in a bubble where she wasn't about to be jailed for the rest of her life.

"Perhaps just a sweet tea for the vicar," Bunch suggested, to Sylvia's evident ire, though the housekeeper was wise enough to keep any comment to herself.

Daisy quietly took a seat at the table, expecting at any

moment a heavy, ginger ball of fluff to land on her lap. When none did, she looked around the room, eventually spotting Jacob sitting watching her intently from the door to the boot room. Whether the cat could sense her unease, her distress even, or whether she was simply out of favour since she hadn't been the one feeding the greedy freeloader recently, Daisy didn't know. Nor, to be honest, did she care. The longer the animals stayed out of the kitchen, the better for poor Gerald's sinuses.

Barely had the tea been poured and an attempt at stilted conversation made then the sound of the new doorbell filled the hallway. Following Bunch's previous explanation to the letter, Sylvia used the app in her phone to see who was on the doorstep.

"I'm not expecting the bishop for another hour," Daisy said, the panic in her chest beginning to bubble and burst to life, "I only came early to pack some more things and…"

"It's okay, love, it's Cluero," Bunch said, peering over Sylvia's shoulder, "I'll let the man in, he might have some updates on the case."

At the mere mention of 'the case' Daisy's body recoiled in physical loathing of the word and everything it represented – her whole life being taken and turned upside down in one night. Sweat gathered in her hairline and on her palms, bile rose up her throat and her breathing became laboured.

"Hey lass, he's one of the good'uns," Sylvia stroked the vicar's back, her voice laced with concern, but the words barely permeated the thick fog in Daisy's head.

Returning to the room with the Welshman in tow, Bunch took one look at Daisy and excused them both for a minute, leaving Sylvia to make the detective a coffee while he himself guided the vicar down to her bedroom.

As if on automatic pilot, Daisy allowed herself to be led, put up no resistance when encouraged to sit on the bed, using the small step stool to get onto the high mattress. In some ways it was all so unchanged, so familiar, yet in others Daisy felt as if she were on a different planet.

"You're okay, love, I've got you, it's just us, you can let it out," Gerald rubbed her back in soothing circles, having learned by now the way her panic attacks usually progressed.

Daisy seemed to take a large breath in and held it for a few seconds before the sobbing started. No quiet build up, just an immediate storm which wracked her body as she took shelter in her friend's arms. Gerald's words managed to penetrate the thick wall of her fear and panic, whispering reassurance and promising support, but more than anything else which she heard through the echo chamber of her grief, was that he believed her. Bunch believed that Daisy was innocent, and that alone gave her strength. Maybe not strength enough to fight, not yet anyway. But enough to wash her face in the small, chipped basin, to force her quaking body to still, and to agree to go back to the kitchen to hear what the detective had to say.

Baby steps.

5. NO REST FOR THE WICKED

Despite his many years on the force, Detective Inspector Rhys Cluero found himself unable to school his features as Daisy Bloom re-entered the vicarage kitchen. He knew that his shock at the change in the vicar, even after just one week, was plastered all over his expression and that knowledge caused him to blush hotly, unable to speak past the lump in his throat. Yet, speak he must, as several things about this investigation just didn't add up. Not to him personally, anyway, his bosses were a different matter. As long as they had enough to get a prosecution the powers that be were happy. It was never personal, simply justice at work. Cluero himself, however, felt personally invested in this case, not least because his own partner was the victim. Not that he'd liked Matlock, but still, she didn't deserve to die. And nor did this lovely woman, who'd dedicated her life to the service of others, deserve to be put away for the crime. No, Cluero was certain that Daisy was innocent, and he intended to do everything within his power to help her prove that. On the down low, of course.

"I'm, ah, not here officially," Cluero began hesitantly, keen not to get any hopes up as he cleared his throat in an effort to return confidence to his voice, "so I hope you don't mind me popping round, off the record, so to speak."

"Not at all," Daisy attempted a smile to put the man at ease, but the most she could manage was to hold her tears in.

"Do you have any news?" Bunch sounded impatient, "Anything that can help Daisy?"

"Gerald," Daisy laid a calming hand on her friend's arm.

"Not news as such, but I do have some thoughts on the matter that may turn into lines of enquiry, unofficially of course."

"Oh?" Daisy tried to be interested, really she did, but her head hurt from the crying and the aftershock of the panic attack, and her hip throbbed. So intricately linked to any stress in her body, her disabilities had been repeatedly triggered this past week and she'd relied heavily on her prescription painkillers. They, of course, came with their own side effects, so focusing on conversation was not the vicar's strong suit right now.

"Well, maybe we can start with the murder weapon," Cluero began, flicking the switch back into professional mode, "Mrs. Carmichael, I believe you told my colleague and then confirmed in your signed statement that the kitchen knife in question definitely came from the vicarage?"

Sylvia cast an apologetic look at Daisy before speaking at half her normal volume, just above a whisper in fact, "I did, yes and it was, yes."

"And how could you be so sure? If you don't mind me asking," Cluero continued in his gentle Welsh lilt.

"Well, a cook likes their own things, you see, and it was part of a set I brought with me when I moved in here. The vicarage had a blunt paring knife and a bread knife, nothing at all for meat, so I brought my own. They were part of a gift from my late husband Ron a while back, each of the handles has a small rabbit carved into the wood. Very distinctive. I'm so sorry," the housekeeper put her head in her hands, shoulders shaking.

Daisy attempted to stand so as to go to the woman and soothe her. When her body refused to cooperate, the vicar ended up staying put and saying, "It's not your fault, Sylvia, nothing at all rests at your feet. Not any of it."

"Indeed," Cluero agreed, "but can any of you shed light on how the murderer acquired the weapon. Had you noticed it missing, Mrs. Carmichael?"

"No lad, I only really used it for roast dinners, and what with the heat it'd been about three weeks since I'd cooked that meal. It could have gone any time since."

"And neither of you noticed any signs of forced entry? Nothing else missing?"

"No, not apart from the vicar here's phone. That caused a lot of disruption, didn't it Daisy? All your contacts missing, your mobile calendar. I told them down at the station that it'd been lost when they kept asking about it."

Cluero's eyes brightened as the housekeeper linked the two missing items, which had hitherto been two separate entries on his mental checklist.

"Quite so, Mrs. Carmichael, quite so. And do you have any idea when your phone went missing, Daisy? Can you narrow down the timeframe from the three weeks we have for the knife?"

"Well, it was definitely the week leading up to the… the, ah, incident. The Wednesday, I think as it was before Sylvia left for Scarbrough. She and I searched high and low because I was sure I'd had it when I came home from the journalling for wellness group the previous evening."

"And it hasn't turned up since?" Cluero asked.

"No."

"And did you have any visitors either that Wednesday evening or on the Thursday before Mrs. Carmichael left?"

"I don't think so," Daisy wracked her foggy brain to drag something out of her memory, "Oh! Just the new curate, popped round to introduce himself."

"And his name is?" Cluero pushed, notebook on the table and pen in hand.

"John Smith," Daisy said, thinking nothing of it.

Cluero and Bunch exchanged a glance but stayed quiet

as Sylvia added, "Nice chap, asked me to get my knitting out when I told him about the blanket I'm working on."

Cluero sighed heavily, "Well, I probably shouldn't disclose this, and it didn't come from me if you're asked, but the text message sent to the victim, Detective Matlock, asking her to meet you by your car, definitely came from you old, I mean your usual number, Vicar. So, if someone had your original handset, then…"

"They could use it to pretend to be me," Daisy finished for him, "I felt like I was going mad when I couldn't find that thing. Still do, to be honest. And the thought of someone being in the vicarage without us knowing…"

"Well, I didn't say that exactly," Cluero continued, his pen tapping on the tabletop, "with no signs of forced entry, no valuables missing… Let me make some enquiries and get back to you in the next day or so."

Time seemed to have no meaning to Daisy any longer and she simply nodded and thanked the man before Bunch saw him out. The two men had a quick, mumbled conversation in the hallway, but the vicar was too tired to strain her ears to hear it. Sylvia, too, looked drained and for once wasn't on her own phone updating her book club friends. Instead, the two women sat in silence, each deep in their own thoughts, until Bunch returned accompanied by the bishop.

"I found Bishop Althorp coming up the path as I let the detective out," Bunch's enthusiasm was obviously forced and his voice came out unusually high pitched.

"No rest for the wicked," Bishop Althorp said, before catching Daisy's eye and immediately regretting his choice of words, "I mean, ah, the Devil makes work for idle hands. Oh! No, no, I just mean you've had a busy morning. Argh, how are you, Daisy?"

6. EVERY CLOUD HAS A SILVER LINING

Bishop Bob Althorp was a large man, used to indulging in the few excesses which his position allowed. Rumour had it that he had a particular fondness for sherry, brandy and bourbon… any strong spirit, in fact, a detail his bulbous red nose and tremorous hands would attest to. He was a man who preferred a simple life, nothing to rock the boat so to speak. Having been widowed some six years earlier, he preferred to live in peace and prayer regularly accompanied by his much younger housekeeper, Honey. Certainly, the man of God was happiest when he had no dealings with the Archbishops' Council, especially on Tuesdays and Thursdays when Honey worked her magic – 'Out of sight, out of mind' was one of his favourite idioms, of which Bishop Bob had many!

This whole murder arrest thing, though, this he couldn't shove under the carpet, couldn't keep under the radar. It had pushed the bishop straight into the limelight in fact, and made his diocese the talk of the upper echelons of clergy. He certainly didn't want anyone looking too closely at how he ran things. No, this attention was something that Bob needed to address post haste, not least before he become tarred with the same brush as his unfortunate subordinate.

To that end, the bishop firmly intended to be in and out in the least amount of time as was charitable under the circumstances. *Better to rip the plaster off,* he told himself as he surveyed the three pairs of eyes watching him intently.

"So, ah, Daisy, might it be better to speak privately?" Bishop Bob began, "Where you can make a full confession?"

"Confession?" Bunch asked, his eyes narrowed and hands fisted on the table, "Why would she want to do that when she's innocent?"

"Well, ah, quite so," the bishop's large jowls jiggled as

he mopped the sweat from his purple brow, "innocent until proven guilty, quite so, quite so. So, ah, what to do, Daisy Bloom? Should I leave you to bloom where you've been planted or uproot you once again? I admit, I must take some responsibility for sending you back here to Lillymouth in the first place. I thought it would help you to move on, to be back here in the bosom of your hometown and to see that Lillymouth wasn't still full of the shadows of your past but, ah, that doesn't seem to have been the case. I do get rather regular correspondence from certain of your parishioners requesting your removal from your post, and that was even before the murder allegations."

"Tea, Bishop?" Sylvia slammed the heavy teapot down on the table and shoved a mug beside it. Had they had a 'best' tea set she certainly wouldn't have wasted it on this apparently esteemed visitor. He had already helped himself to a large piece of the carrot cake, sans plate, which had been shovelled in in record time, the crumbled remains now scattered across his stained shirt.

"So, have you come to a decision?" Daisy's voice was a strained monotone, no emotion slipping through whatsoever. Beneath the table, though, her knee bounced up and down in anxious agitation until she felt Bunch's large hand rest there and soothe her with his gently massaging fingers.

"Well, the decision wasn't necessarily mine, you see, it came from above. Doesn't everything?" He rubbed the large cross which hung around his neck rolls and sent his eyes heavenward in pious reverence. Bunch let out a large sigh that bordered on a growl.

"So, I have been removed from my position here," Daisy filled in the blanks for him. Not that she wanted to let the man off the hook, but rather to get this awful visit over with as quickly as possible.

"You will be paid your notice, of course, and have a month to move out. Remember, Daisy, every cloud has a silver lining. With the experience you're getting now you'll be able to empathise with others all the better."

"What? The falsely accused and the homeless? I was hoping my experience after my grandmother's death would be sufficient to equip me in that area!" Daisy's voice was full of all the emotion she had hitherto held back.

"Now Daisy, the grass is greenest where you water it," the man was visibly uncomfortable now, half standing as if to make a quick exit, but not before grabbing a second piece of Sylvia's homemade cake for the journey home, "when all this blows over you can make a fresh start somewhere else."

"In prison, for example," Daisy replied bitterly, "but of course, your duty is done Bob and how fortuitous you have the new curate starting next week."

"New curate?" His bushy eyebrows squashed together in perplexed brotherhood, "New curate? No my dear, this is going to cause me quite a lot of extra work and organisation to cover you, I can tell you. There's no one new on the horizon to help me out."

"Should we be sympathetic?" Sylvia asked, though she was drowned out by the scraping of Daisy's chair as she pushed it urgently back and rushed to the sink.

Immediately, Gerald was there rubbing her back, "It's okay love, it's all going to be okay."

"He wasn't a real curate, was he?" Daisy choked on the words.

"I'm thinking not, love, and I got the impression Cleuro suspected as much too."

"Well, goodbye Daisy, the night is always darkest just before the dawn," Bishop Bob added unhelpfully as he saw himself out.

"If I wasn't in uniform, I'd..." Archie added his

sentiments from the boot room, setting the cat off yowling.

Daisy's head swam amidst the cacophony of noise and she felt dizziness encroaching as Gerald helped her back to her seat whilst Sylvia passed her a glass of water.

"Is he always so full of platitudes and clichés?" The housekeeper asked, "Why doesn't he quote bible verses instead?"

"I doubt he can remember any, the stupid lump of lard," Bunch replied, his face a mixture of anger and concern, "he's hardly representative of Christian love and charity."

Whether the man was aware of his own contradiction in those two statements, Daisy didn't know, but she was sure that Gerald Bunch was ten times the man the bishop was.

"So, I'd better get packed," the vicar began, standing again as if she couldn't bear to be sitting doing nothing, though her whole body slumped in defeat with only her walking stick seeming to hold her up at all.

"You'll do no such thing," Sylvia chided, "we're going

to find this killer and have you reinstated. You were obviously set up. We just need to figure out by whom."

"I think that may be easier said than done," Daisy whispered, "but I appreciate the support."

"Would you like to have a lie down or get back home... I mean to the florist's?" Bunch asked.

"I think I might just grab a few things and leave town for a while..." Daisy began.

"No you will not!" The stern voice came from the doorway, "You really need to make sure that door is closed and locked," Joe glared at Bunch, "You ran away once before Daisy Bloom and I'll be damned if I'm letting you do it again. You're innocent, every decent neighbour knows it, and by goodness we're going to prove it."

7. A GLOW UP

"And don't get me started on the way you've been avoiding me and letting Bunch here keep everyone at arm's length," Joe continued as he strode in and took a seat at the table.

"We'll need another pot of tea," Sylvia said decisively, as if they were preparing for a war council, which Daisy supposed in a way they were. Not that she had any energy for it.

"And while we're on the subject of you, Mr. Bunch, what is it with the complete change of character? It's not just your appearance, it's your voice, your attitude to my Daisy here. Now I'm not complaining, since you seem much more respectful and a lot less lecherous, but, ah…"

"I guess you could call it a glow up," Daisy answered for the florist, who looked extremely uncomfortable.

"What's that? Like light therapy or summat?" Joe looked perplexed.

Daisy stifled a smile, the first in many days or so it felt, "No, Joe, I suppose you would call it becoming the best version of himself." This time she did smile properly, an expression full of pure admiration which was directed straight at Gerald and didn't go unnoticed by the older man who had known her since she was a toddler.

When Yorkshire's finest had been poured from the hefty teapot and Rich Tea biscuits passed round, Joe addressed the serious matter at hand, "Well, I've been to the main station at Whitby…"

"What?" Daisy couldn't help but interrupt, "Why Joe?"

"Why do you think? To tell them they've made a big mistake. That you've obviously been set up and they need to drop all charges before I sue them! Not that it did any good. Got myself escorted out of the station by that Daniel Harper of all people – Bea's dad, isn't he? –

miserable bloke, always scowling, wouldn't even hear me out," Joe noticed Daisy's own scowl and hurried on, "anyway, we need to put our heads together, the four of us here, and think who might have set you up."

"Well, we might've had a breakthrough there actually," Bunch spoke for the first time since Joe's arrival, "since it turns out the visit Daisy had from a curate the other week wasn't actually a curate at all."

"What do you mean, not a curate? What is he then, another vicar? One of those Arch-whatsits?" Joe had no idea what other ranks and ordinations existed within the Church of England, nor had he ever had any inclination to find out.

"No, you're missing the point," Sylvia sounded exasperated, "he was the typical dodgy underling doing the undercover shifty stuff." Clearly prime time cop shows provided an excellent education in the ways of the crime underworld.

Joe looked none the wiser so Daisy helped him out, "He wasn't sent by the bishop at all. He was a fraud. But he seemed so convincing. I mean, I did wonder why he insisted Sylvia come to get me from my church office instead of meeting me there. Now I suppose it was so he could have five minutes alone in the kitchen to steal the knife."

"What? He was right here and you were both in danger?" Joe asked, spluttering the words.

"I doubt we were in danger," Sylvia replied matter-of-factly, "that wasn't part of the grand plan, was it? It would do no good if he aroused suspicions."

"So how did he get your phone?" Joe continued, his worry lines deep across his forehead.

Daisy looked pointedly at the phone resting beside her on the kitchen table, the new, cheap handset she had bought to replace the 'lost' one, "Well, I guess I have a habit of sitting it here beside me, so when Sylvia went to get her knitting to show the man – at his clever request – he probably waited for me to nip into the boot room to quieten the animals, or to pop to the bedroom for my diary. Whatever, he only needed a couple of seconds."

"Wow. Okay, okay, so he was definitely working for someone. Someone who wanted to set you up for murder. So we need to figure out who," Joe ran his fingers through his hair, for once looking every year of his age. Daisy hadn't seen him like this since the days after Gran's murder and she felt immediately guilty for putting everyone through this.

"Well the obvious suspects would be Robert Briggs, for

the way Daisy had his son put away for murder, and Violet Glendinning, for, ah, the same reason," Sylvia was either making notes on her phone like any good detective or live messaging her book club ladies about the updates. Daisy didn't really care at this point. She knew she was the hot topic of gossip around the town, and quite honestly that was the last of her worries right now.

"Backtracking for a moment," Bunch said, "what about this imposter curate, wouldn't his fingerprints be on the knife drawer?"

"Oh! I hadn't thought of that," Daisy sent him a grateful smile, "I'd have noticed if he was wearing gloves in the middle of summer… in fact, I'm pretty sure he wasn't because Jacob took an instant dislike to the man and clawed his hand the first chance he got."

"I'll get Cluero to ask someone to come over and dust the place," the florist replied, getting his own phone out of his pocket. Since when he had the local detective on speed dial Daisy could only imagine, and for a brief moment she wondered what discussions they'd had without her. She hated feeling like a child.

"No, I'll speak to him myself in a minute," Daisy said firmly and was glad when for once Bunch put up no resistance, "anyway, on the topic of who would set me up, I've had a lot of time to think about that and I need to ask you all, right now, to not do any more digging… please. It will only put you all in danger and I can't have that. I mean, I've been asking around, hunting for Gran's murderer since my return. What if I've poked the beast and now they want me out of the way?"

"Well why wouldn't they just kill you?" Sylvia asked, before blushing hotly as she received a harsh glare from Joe.

"That I can't figure out," Daisy replied, "there must be more to it, but what?"

"Anyway," Joe said, "no one will be getting murdered, because there's no way you're doing this alone, right Bunch?"

"Right," Gerald nodded, "I don't mean to hurt you Daisy, but you, ah, haven't been coping so well. Locking yourself away will not help find whoever set you up. I'm with Joe on this one, I'm afraid, we need to work as a team and give you all the support we can. No going it alone." He sent a smile and a wink in Daisy's direction to soften the words, but still she felt her back stiffen.

"I'm not a child, Gerald!" Daisy bit out.

"I'm very well aware of that," the man replied, his eyes darkening and heat rising up his neck. For a moment it seemed as if it were just the two of them in the room and Daisy felt her own body heating up in awareness.

"Anyway," Joe drew the word out, looking from one to the other thoughtfully.

"Do you know why my Gran was afraid of my birth father?" Daisy blurted out.

Shocked silence greeted her from both Joe and Sylvia, and not just at the sudden change in subject.

"Well, ah, how do you know that she wa…" Joe began, causing Daisy to cut him off.

"Oh come on, Sylvia here gets the shakes and goes pale whenever I bring up the topic and you always change the subject. It was what Gran and I had been arguing about in the days that led up to her death. I'd got my birth certificate, seen there was no father's name listed, and was demanding she give me the details. So, I need to know. Was he a criminal? Did he threaten Gran? Hold something over her? Was my mum afraid of him? I've been wondering after the events with Tallie and Anthony Glendinning whether my mother's hit and run was actually an accident, or was it planned in advance like theirs was?" Daisy took a deep breath, thankful that she'd got all of that off her chest as it had been festering there for a while.

"Well, yes, if we're being honest and I suppose now is the time to be, then yes Wendy was afraid. I've never seen her keep a secret so steadfastly. In fact, I really believe it was the only thing she refused to share with me and I have to admit it did come between us at times," Joe's eyes were full of sadness at the memories, "I met your grandmother a couple of years after you were born, just before your mum died, Daisy, and I never knew who your dad was. But believe me, I wish I had. I don't know what hold he had over the two of them, what kept their silence, but I can tell you now I don't think you should go digging in that area. Focus on finding who set you up for murder, maybe you'll even uncover your grandmother's killer in the process. For goodness sakes though leave it to Bunch and me to speak to Briggs and Glendinning, you know what they can be like."

"No! Any speaking to will be done by me!" Daisy's voice was high pitched now in her effort to get her point across and it set the animals off in the adjoining room, "I'm not a child who needs sheltering from harsh realities or difficult situations!" Bunch and Joe shared a look, to which Daisy glared at them in response.

"Daisy, petal," Sylvia tried to soothe, "your Gran didn't tell me who your dad was either but yes, Joe's right, she was very afraid of the man. Could he have killed your mother? Your Gran believed he could, she even said as much to the police I think, but got nowhere. I really think you should do as Joe says and consider that a dead end. As for the rest, I know you want to do this by yourself, but to be honest we're all already involved, aren't we? The curate bloke knows I could recognise him as well as you could, anyone can see how close you are to Gerald here, and Joe has already tried to storm the castle in Whitby, so asking us to back off now is a bit like closing the stable door after the horse has bolted."

"Now you sound like the bishop," Daisy forced a smile, "but I hear you. I also know that if I'm insisting none of you act on my behalf then I need to force myself to go out and about as if I have nothing to be ashamed of. Like I'm innocent, which I am, even if my anxiety kills me in the process."

"Your anxiety won't kill you, love, and you won't be going out alone," Bunch said gently.

"Aye, maybe if we're all asking questions publicly we'll ruffle the right feathers and the guilty party will expose themselves," Sylvia agreed.

"You're not doing anything to put yourself in danger though, lass," Joe looked at Daisy pointedly.

"Love you all," Daisy whispered, wiping the single tear that ran down her cheek.

"And we love you," Joe said, his own eyes suddenly glassy, "but no group hugs, eh?"

They all tried to laugh but the moment was too emotional for levity. Instead, Daisy nodded through her tears, so grateful for her found family, a blessing indeed.

8. KNOWLEDGE IS POWER

Daisy knew she could just stay at the vicarage with Sylvia, but for reasons she didn't want to admit even to herself she chose to remain at the florist's, for the moment at least. Of course, Bunch had no issue whatsoever with that, seemed delighted in fact, and suggested they grab some posh sandwiches from the deli at the bottom of Cobble Wynd for a late lunch on their way back from the vicarage. Daisy hesitated at first, the thought of walking down the small town's main shopping street did not fill her with joy. Quite the opposite in fact. But she needed to put her money where her mouth was, so to speak, so she pulled up her metaphorical big girl knickers and agreed that it would be a lovely idea.

What the pair found, of course, was that whilst a few people did stare briefly and a couple of older ladies did have a quiet whisper, by and large most people were too busy going about their own daily lives to care that the disgraced vicar had come out of hibernation. It wasn't until they had almost made it to their intended destination at the bottom of the cobbled street that Daisy heard her name being called. She froze on the spot with the hand that had already been linked in Bunch's arm now squeezing him almost painfully.

Bunch turned first, with Daisy slower to see the owner of the voice. She needn't have worried though, and had the vicar actually allowed herself to be more focused on her surroundings rather than head down, scuttling along, she would have recognised Bea's voice.

"Daisy, I've been trying to catch up with you, but the pushchair doesn't work so well on the cobbles!" Her friend exclaimed, "How are you? Would you like to come to the Book Nook for a coffee and cake? On the house of course. We've had a lovely, steady trade since the train launch day, all thanks to you. I've missed you, you haven't been answering my texts, and I know how you persevered with me when I was in the depths of postnatal depression. Let's have a catch up now, please?"

Despite the heartfelt plea from her oldest friend, Daisy really wanted to say no, wanted to crawl back into her hole, but before she could think of an excuse to let Bea down gently, Bunch answered for them both, "That would be lovely. We haven't had lunch yet."

"Well then that's perfect," Bea set off ahead with little Daisy Mae in the misbehaving buggy, whose wheels jittered along bumping first one way and then the other, whilst Daisy sent a glare to the tall man beside her as her cane tapped brusquely on the cobbles.

"In for a penny, in for a pound as Bishop Bob would say," Gerald winked and tucked the vicar's arm back in his as they made their way to the bottom corner of Cobble Wynd and Bea's Book Nook.

Daisy had to admit that there was nothing better than snuggling the little girl who had celebrated her first birthday a few months ago. Daisy Mae was so interactive now, and so wriggly that she had Daisy bouncing her on her lap and reading to her in no time. The scent of books, leather and coffee was a familiar comfort to the vicar who had sat in this same spot so many times since she was a young girl herself. Bunch watched the pair quietly, a wistful look on his face and a hint of sadness in his eyes as Bea bustled about making the coffees and preparing a plate of sandwiches and cakes, chatting away about the projects that Andrew had been offered after renovating the old train station.

"So, how are you, really?" Bea asked when Daisy Mae had been encouraged into her play pen in the corner with a pile of soft toys and board books, so that the adults could eat in peace.

"Um, about as well as you'd expect," Daisy answered, "when you've been labelled a murderer and apparently don't have any say in the matter." She tried but failed to keep the bitterness from her voice.

"No one believes it you know. I mean, other than Violet and her cronies, everyone that's been in has said how terrible it is and how they know you would never…" Bea stopped mid-sentence, seeing the look on Daisy's face. They could read each other so well, having been friends since they were children despite the small blip earlier in the year, "Anyway, I hear you have moved in with Gerald here?" She gave a cheeky wink and Daisy felt herself blushing even though she knew she was being teased.

"You know fine well that I'm in the spare room," Daisy replied, unable to stifle her smile. One glance at Bunch, however, and she saw how uncomfortable the teasing made him so once again changed the subject,

"Actually, Bea, I was going to call you. You know what Joe's like, and I think he went to police headquarters all guns blazing, but he mentioned your dad was there and it gave me an idea. I mean, I know he's never liked us being friends, but since he's chief constable or whatever the proper title is, I was wondering if he could look into the archives for me? I really need to know who the investigating officers were on my mum's hit and run case and for gran's murder."

"Why Daisy? I mean, I can ask him but, ah, well, you know how he is about mixing work and personal life. But really, is it a good idea to delve into all that again? I want to help you, you know I do, but I'm guessing your anxiety is at an all-time high. Is it wise to bring up all those emotions again?"

"I doubt it, to be honest, but I just need information. Knowledge is power, as they say, and I feel the more information I have the more likely I might be to see a pattern, or a piece of the puzzle, or something. I don't know. I guess Gran's murder file will be computerized but mum's hit and run was thirty years ago so that'll be a paper file somewhere. If your dad could check? Any information would be great, really."

Bea didn't look convinced but she nodded before shooting a worried look at Bunch once Daisy was distracted by the toddler once more. The florist himself simply smiled, no doubt reassured that Daisy was regaining some of her confidence and taking control back.

Forcing herself to partake in the social contact that she had recently been avoiding at all costs took it out of Daisy, so the visit was short and sweet and they were back at the florist's less than an hour later.

"I'm so tired," Daisy whispered as they sat on the sofa, "maybe just a quick nap."

"Take as long as you need," Bunch replied, handing her a glass of water for her painkillers and sitting down next to Daisy.

He had expected her to go to her room to snooze, so the man was surprised when the vicar instead curled into his side and snuggled close, bringing with her the scents of coconut and roses which he had come to associate with his lodger. His lodger who was at once just that and at the same time so much more.

"Will you undo my braid? It's too tight and digging in," Daisy whispered, already half asleep.

Gerald wanted to grab a blanket from the spare

bedroom to make her as warmly cocooned and comfortable as possible, but didn't want to disturb the gloriously cosy moment, so instead he pulled his jacket from the arm of the sofa and laid it over the vicar before gently removing the hair bobble and unplaiting her hair. He was glad that Daisy couldn't see how his hands shook to be doing something for her that felt so intimate, and allowed himself only a moment of running his fingers through the silky blonde strands before he put his arm around the woman he would give his life to protect and allowed his own eyes to drift closed.

9. A LUCKY CHARM

It was late when they both awoke. Afternoon had turned into evening and there was a chill in the air. Still half asleep and only vaguely aware of her surroundings, Daisy snuggled closer into Gerald's warmth, feeling his arm tighten around her shoulders. The sleeping position had not been kind to her hip and side, which grumbled under her skin, but for once Daisy didn't care that she always awoke in pain. Didn't care that she had wasted what was left of the day. For it had been the deepest, most nightmare-free sleep she had had in a very long time.

"Alright love?" Bunch asked, smiling down at her, his own features soft with sleep. He must've taken his glasses off to doze, because his eyes looked bigger than

Daisy had ever seen them. So beautiful. Without overthinking, she reached her hand up to stroke his cheek, tilting her face to look at him directly.

Bunch swallowed audibly, running his spare hand through his hair which he'd allowed to grow longer in recent weeks and leaving it sticking up in all directions, "I'd, ah, better get cooking, ah…"

"No, don't rush off," Daisy whispered, not taking her fingers off his face. Her hand seemed to have a mind of its own, tracing the outline of his features from his temple to his jaw and then across his lips.

"Daisy, please," it was a plea, a desperate request that she cease her gentle touches and allow him to move before…

It was actually the vicar whose actions couldn't be trusted, whose self-control was compromised. Daisy was aware of this, and also very sure that she didn't care a jot about all the reasons she'd told herself in the past why this wasn't a good idea. All simply excuses at the end of the day. So, she reached her face towards his, her eyes smiling up at Gerald's shocked ones until Daisy lowered her lids at the moment their lips touched. It was only a featherlight brush, a barely-there meeting. Nevertheless, Daisy felt it deeply and if Bunch's sharp intake of breath was anything to go by, so did he.

It ended all too fast, as Gerald pulled away. Reluctant to break the skin to skin connection, Daisy ran her thumb along his cheekbone, smiling reassuringly.

"Daisy," his voice was a gruff croak and he tried again, "Daisy, if this isn't what you want. If it's the stress or the situation then that's okay, but if so please stop now. It's easy for feelings to become confused when…"

"Please stop talking, Marcus," Daisy whispered, using Bunch's real name to shock him into silence, "and kiss me. When it comes down to it, I'm not sure why I've been denying us both this connection, this pleasure for so long. It's as if I'd decided I was unable of feeling a certain way back when I was in my early twenties and then refused to acknowledge that like all people, I'm capable of changing. Since I do feel that way right here and now. And I do, Marcus, I do feel that way about you. Please let me kiss you." It had come out a bit jumbled but judging by the darkening of desire in the man's eyes he'd understood just fine.

It was a small growl from deep in his chest that proceeded Caldwell's lips crashing down onto Daisy's right then. Forceful but soft. Gentle yet demanding, he kissed her with all the love that he had been burying deep inside himself. Much like the buried treasure he still sought, the discovery was all the sweeter for the search it had taken him on.

Daisy had never been kissed like that, not in her whole life – though, to be fair, she didn't have much to compare it to. But as far as kisses go, the ones that you can feel right down to your toes, it took her breath away in the best possible way.

"Is this okay?" Marcus checked again, pulling away before claiming her lips once more at Daisy's quick nod. His fingers tangled in her hair while hers played with his hairline at the back of his neck, holding him to her.

"I could kiss you like that for hours," Daisy whispered several minutes later, "and I intend to, though I've been wondering if you'd take me to the beach? It's my favourite place and I've been avoiding it despite metaphorically burying my head in the sand."

"Oh! Well, yes, of course, if you think you're up for another walk? Or I could bring the car round."

"No, I didn't mean going the public way," Daisy waited for him to catch her drift.

"You want to go in the tunnels?"

"I do, I want to see what they're like, what's been

driving you all these years. Besides, it'll be like our secret passageway."

"You make it sound romantic, love, when really it's cramped and muddy. You'll probably get away with just lowering your head, but..."

"It's okay, I want to. I can bring my stick and I'll have you to guide me and keep me upright. You never know, I might be a lucky charm and find you some treasure."

The man didn't look convinced. In fact, his eyes were still love-glazed and his brain hadn't kicked properly back into gear yet. In this moment, it's likely there was nothing he would deny this woman if it were at all within the realms of his ability, "Okay then, let's eat first and wait until it's properly dark, then we'll have an adventure."

"Perfect," Daisy whispered, sealing the deal with another kiss or three.

The tunnel was indeed overly moist and smelly, and Daisy didn't want to think about the creatures and insects that lived down there. Gerald – as she was determined to think of him when they weren't being cosy together – had lent her his only hardhat complete with headtorch, whilst he had a large handheld light which shone a bright beam far ahead. Even with her stick, Daisy stumbled repeatedly on the uneven ground and more than once Bunch suggested they turn back. The vicar was nothing if not stubborn, however, and insisted they continue, glad that Bunch had lamps dotted along the route that he lit when they came to them, illuminating the tunnel with a yellow glow. The marks of years of digging, of scraping back the walls, were evident as Daisy studied her narrow surroundings. Her stick bashed repeatedly on the wall which was close to the side of her foot, and a few times she actually tripped on the walking aid, but all in all they reached the entrance to the beach caves without any injury.

Bunch had checked the tide times, as he always did before venturing down into the basement of the florist's shop and into the tunnels which ran from there to the shore. Thankfully it was currently low tide, so they emerged into the dank, dark depths of the cave with only sand and rocks stretching out between them and the North sea. Daisy took a moment to breathe in the salty goodness, the air which she always found both restorative and rejuvenating. They were both slightly breathless from the trek as Gerald put his arms around her and snuggled Daisy against his chest.

"I guess I wasn't your lucky treasure charm," Daisy said, though to be fair she'd had too much to think about to avoid falling over as she'd walked along to even consider studying the ground and walls with sufficient focus to look for treasure.

"I have a feeling I've all the treasure I need right here," Bunch whispered against her hair.

"You're so corny, but I love you for it," Daisy said, reaching onto her tiptoes to kiss him.

"Do you?" Gerald asked when they finally broke apart.

"Do I what?"

"Love me?"

"I think I do, yes," and instead of feeling anxious at the admission, Daisy's heart felt more at peace than it perhaps ever had.

10. FARM

Well, the life of Daisy Bloom could never be accused of being a romance novel, so of course the pair returned to reality with a bang when they got back to the shop to find Detective Cluero on the doorstep.

So much for hot cocoa and a long bath, Daisy thought to herself, disappointed that their bubble had been burst so soon.

"Twice in one day, Detective, you're spoiling us," Bunch said as he let the man in, only remembering at the last minute to remind Daisy to take off her hardhat.

If the Welshman was shocked by their dishevelled, muddy appearance, he refrained from comment, instead saying, "I hope it's not too late, I did try to call first. In fact, I was about to give up when there was no response from hammering on the window."

"Not at all," Daisy replied, "did you get the message I left with Ornsley about the fake curate?"

"No, sorry, but I have been in and out all day."

"You weren't at the station and I thought it needed to be dealt with urgently so I asked to speak to Ornsley and told him about the possibility of fingerprints in the vicarage kitchen, left by the guy masquerading as a clergyman when he was stealing the knife and my phone. I asked him to pass on the message so you could arrange someone to come out asap, or better still to make the arrangements himself," Daisy shuddered at the memory of having to speak to that awful man again. Needs must though if she was going to clear her name, so Daisy had forced herself to go through with the conversation before they left the vicarage earlier that day.

"Strange, I saw him several times over the course of the afternoon and he never mentioned it. Let me check if he just went ahead and organised the fingerprint analyst to go out. Did you tell Mrs. Carmichael to avoid cleaning and to steer clear of the knife drawer in the meantime?" Cluero already had his phone in hand.

Daisy nodded that she had indeed left such instructions with her housekeeper before she and Bunch headed upstairs to the living area, the detective following them as he spoke in low tones.

"So?" Bunch asked when Cluero had finished his call. The man's eyes were sunken in the dark circles which surrounded them and his face weary.

"No, actually, very strange, no record of your call is in the case notes and nothing has been actioned. I've given instructions for someone to come out to the vicarage first thing in the morning. Ornsley is a senior chap in the department though, one of my bosses in fact, and he doesn't normally deal hands on with cases any more. I guess he just got involved in this one because it was one of our team that was murdered. Anyway, he likes to give the illusion of being very busy, but whatever he does all day is a mystery. I'm surprised he even took your call, he has underlings to do that. Next time you're better just sending me a text, I'll give you my personal number."

Daisy was grateful for Cluero's efficiency but annoyed at Ornsley. *What was the point in getting involved if you weren't going to do things in a timely manner?* She wondered. *What example is that for your staff? Besides, the odious man had reassured her she could call him about anything to do with the case. That Daisy could bypass his team and contact him directly if anything else came up.*

"Well, it seems you have both reached the conclusion that I was coming here to discuss," Cluero said, after accepting a cup of coffee and a ginger snap, "after our discussion this morning I did some digging, spoke to the parish office at the bishop's residence, and the clerk told me they have no clergyman named John Smith in their records for this area. Nice chap, even phoned around a bit and couldn't locate anyone by that name in the whole of the northern Church of England. Was positive the bishop hadn't been interviewing either, since he said he'd be the one to arrange all of the interviews on behalf of Bishop Althorp. So, we can be sure Smith was an imposter who evidently came to the vicarage undercover to gain your trust and steal what would become incriminating evidence." He took a large gulp of the hot coffee, spilling a little on his tie which looked as if it suffered the same fate several times a day, judging by the dark brown stains which covered the faded maroon stripes.

"I just don't know how I could've been so stupid. Between the curate and the boy who knocked for help, why didn't I suspect anything?" Daisy mused out loud, determined to not let herself get upset again.

"How about because you're a vicar, it's your job to help people. And a guy who's posing as a colleague, well, most people would take that on face value if their job was within the church. You just see the best in people, love, nothing wrong with that," Bunch smiled at Daisy reassuringly from the armchair opposite the sofa which she shared with the detective.

"Exactly," Cluero agreed, "whoever's behind this played on your trusting nature, Daisy, it's nothing you should feel embarrassed about. I'll need you to call me tomorrow morning though so we can arrange for you to give a description of the man to one of our artists. Then we'll have a better idea exactly who we're looking for."

"But who is behind it?" Daisy mused, "Who hired someone to play that part? Who even gave a statement saying they saw me commit murder, because that person is definitely lying too. They must've been recruited into it just like the fake curate. So, how can their statement stand up?"

Cluero looked uncomfortable, then torn, "Well, I have that information, Daisy, but obviously I'm not at liberty to share it. Besides, I can't have you storming up there and scuppering your case by interfering with a witness. That would get your bail revoked and you locked up faster than you can say farm." Cluero's eyes narrowed as if he were calculating whether his point had hit home. But which point exactly, the one about not interfering, or…

"Farm?" Daisy parroted back.

"Farm," Cluero repeated and he and Bunch shared a nod of understanding.

Where Daisy couldn't go demanding answers, the florist could, and there was only one person who owned a farm on the outskirts of the town.

Briggs.

The next morning Bunch's bedroom was empty when Daisy went to give him the cup of tea she'd made. For the first time since she'd come to stay at the florist's, the vicar had managed to get up and dressed in a timely manner, and all without the hot beverage Gerald normally brought her when she couldn't face starting the day.

Well, today Daisy thought she'd surprise the man by beating him to it and yet here she was, cup in hand and packet of biscuits in the other, only to find his bed unmade but empty. Daisy limped down the narrow staircase into the shop, but there was no sign of Bunch there either, just a delivery driver who was about to knock. Daisy did feel bad that the flower shop had been well and truly put on the back burner since her impromptu arrival, so she signed for the beautiful blooms and took a moment to place them in the empty buckets and vases of water which stood right where they always had, right where her gran had been bashed in the head with the same. Daisy shook her head to clear it of the unwanted images and focused on the smell of the dahlias and gladioli. Happy that the place looked a lot less neglected now they had some stock to sell.

By the time she'd done this, checked he wasn't in the basement and double checked the shop door was locked again after the delivery, Daisy had to accept that Gerald wasn't in the building. She wondered if he'd popped out to get them some breakfast, though it would be out of character for him to go out without letting her know, aware as he was that Daisy would be quick to worry.

Annoyed when she realised she'd left her phone on her nightstand and so had potentially missed a text message which would explain everything, Daisy hauled herself back upstairs to the flat, remembering to grab her painkillers from the coffee table before hurrying back into her room. The unease at Bunch's absence was more than an uncomfortable niggle now, it was beginning to turn to panic as Daisy picked up her phone and saw that there were six missed calls and six new voicemails as she'd left the device on silent all night.

Surprisingly, though, and whether for good or bad Daisy wasn't sure, none of them were from Gerald. There had been no contact from that man at all. Instead, every single call was from Sylvia.

Daisy tried hard not to panic, she really did, hitting call back without even bothering to listen to the messages. She ignored her shaking hands, her shallow breaths and her sweaty palms and focussed on the dial tone, which rang only once before Sylvia answered.

"Daisy, thank goodness, are you okay?"

"Yes, of course, it was you who phoned me repeatedly. Are you okay?"

"Aye petal, I was worried they'd got to you too."

"Got to me? What do you mean, Sylvia?" The tunnel vision was pressing in as the dizziness began.

"Did you not listen to my voice messages, lass? The vicarage has been burgled."

11. AN IMPROMPTU TRIP TO THE VET'S

"No, no, no, I should've been there," Daisy began crying. Fat, silent tears which ran unchecked over her now chiselled cheekbones, "What happened? Did they hurt you?"

"Me petal? No, I had my headphones in and a repeat of Traffic Cops on my tablet thingy you got me for Christmas so my old tele wouldn't be blaring at all hours. You know I'm a night owl, don't turn it off till about two in the morning, The first I knew was when Jacob and Archie joined me and Malone in bed. I went down to see how they'd got out of the boot room, and..." the housekeeper's voice wobbled.

"What was it? What did you find?" Her need for all the details was making Daisy shout.

"Well, they must've come in and out through the boot room window, so that's all smashed, and Archie isn't himself at all. I'm not sure if it's glass or what, but I'm guessing I owe those two little loves my life because Terry Stewart says it looks like it was the animals that ran them out of there. There's mess all round the kitchen, the knife drawer's missing…"

"The knife drawer? The one we were about to have forensics check for fingerprints?" Daisy's sharp intake of breath filled the momentary silence.

"Aye petal, I'm so sorry, it's gone," Sylvia whispered through her tears.

"But how could they have known? We didn't tell anyone about that," Daisy began throwing on clothes with her phone on speaker, keen to get to the vicarage as soon as she could. All thoughts of Bunch momentarily forgotten.

"I don't know lass, I'm sorry, I need to get out now to the vet's. I've had hell's own job getting Jacob into the carrier, not least because he obviously hasn't been in it for some time and I've practically had to wedge his bottom in there and it's still squidging out the side slits."

"Hang on a minute and I'll come with you, I'll be there in less than ten minutes," Daisy fought with her dungarees as her mind raced with the implications of this development. Who had been in the room when they were discussing the possibility of fingerprints? Just the four, Sylvia, Joe, Gerald and herself. And she had only told the two detectives, Ornsley and Cluero. But only the Welshman knew that the place was to be dusted for fingerprints first thing the next day, though Daisy supposed it would be on the case files now.

By the time they returned to the vicarage after their impromptu trip to the vet's, both women were in need of a large pot of tea and some late breakfast. Shame the teapot was lying in two pieces on the kitchen floor – Daisy had thought it would take an earthquake to break that thing, but she'd been wrong. All it took was a burglar and two angry animals. As it turned out, Archie had been examined and found to be thankfully free of glass in his little body and feathers, but had been agitated by hair stuck in his beak – hair which belonged to the intruder. No doubt left there as Archie pecked at the unwelcome nighttime visitor. Similarly, Jacob had tiny pieces of the criminal's skin and blood under his sharp claws, evidence which the vet had carefully removed and added to the sterile sample container with the hair, ready for Detective Cluero. Other than that, the vet had said there was nothing at all wrong with the large cat that a strict diet and a personality transplant couldn't sort out.

Shovelling tuna out of the tin and into Jacob's cat bowl like her life depended on it, Daisy was desperate to stop the indignant yowling which the furious feline had begun the moment the vet tried to get him back in the carrier. After a scuffle involving teeth and claws, all involved had decided it was best if the portly animal travelled back in a blanket on the vicar's knee. With the hairs removed from his beak, Archie too had become very vocal, and Daisy's head was throbbing with a migraine. The detective was about to arrive at the vicarage at any moment, and Daisy was in need of his calm, logical manner.

"Here, eat this and be quiet… you little hero," Daisy added the last as an afterthought.

"Aye, they've finally earned their keep," Sylvia agreed, letting Archie free from the travel cage and watching as he flew three circuits of the room.

A hammering on the front door caused all four to freeze in silent pause, still unsettled as they were by the night's events.

"It'll be Cluero, I called and asked him to come but it turns out he has information for us anyways, though I'm not sure what," Daisy whispered, more to calm herself than anyone else, "I'll get it."

It wasn't the detective, though he was due any minute, instead it was Bunch who stood on the doorstep, his eyes wild and blood on his shirt and on the hand which was still raised to knock again.

"I couldn't find you, Daisy. Why did you leave the shop?" The florist's hands shook and his panic was plain to see.

"Gerald!" Daisy pulled the man inside lest anyone else see him in this state. "What on earth has happened? Where were you? Where are you injured?"

"It's not my blood, love," was all the man had time to say as Daisy spotted the detective's car entering the churchyard gates.

"Lord above, what have you done?" Daisy ushered the man into her bedroom and told him to stay put, adding as an afterthought that he could wash as much as possible off in the little sink. "I need to deal with this break-in, but then you're going to tell me everything."

"Break-in? What break-in? Daisy!" It was no use, though, as the vicar was already hobbling back to the kitchen, her head spinning and her breath coming in sharp gasps.

"I've had to put the bags straight in the cups but I've made us some tea," Sylvia said, with all the pride of having solved some great riddle.

"Thank you," Daisy knew her housekeeper must be shaken up, "we just need you to go over it all once more for Cluero, then you can get back to bed."

Sylvia nodded, her hair still in its curlers not moving an inch under her silk headscarf, "Thank you lass, I'll just let the book club ladies know I'm okay." She took out her phone and started typing as Daisy let the detective in.

Cluero looked as well as Daisy felt, which is to say quite ill. The vicar wondered if he ever had a day off, or even a proper meal. She resolved to make the man just that as soon as this ghastly business was all over. Maybe even take him out to a restaurant to say thank you for being at her beck and call throughout one too many murder investigations. Of course, then it hit the vicar that potentially being in prison herself might make that an impossibility, so she turned her focus to the matter at hand.

The detective took a quick look around the kitchen and in the boot room. He didn't seem surprised, but then Daisy had given him a brief synopsis of events over the phone. The cat and bird had been ushered into the sitting room with plenty of food to keep them quiet since the arrival of someone else seemed to tip them over the edge. As Jacob barrelled towards the detective, fur flying and whiskers high above bared teeth, Daisy had thankfully managed to scoop him up – adding injury to insult where her own body was concerned – and take the squirming ginger cannonball to the living room, with Sylvia hurrying behind with his bowl and another can of tuna. Goodness knows how they would ever get the greedy guzzler back on his normal kibble now, but that was a problem for another day. Seeing a bag of his favourite mealworms under Sylvia's arm, the mynah bird had happily flown behind, adding a charming "You're done for!" for good measure. Of course, the house rabbit had been happily ensconced on the armchair by the fire since the early hours, ignoring the local police's visit and apparently oblivious to Sylvia's distress. Now, though, seeing his space invaded, he had charged at Daisy's legs as she tried to place Jacob on the sofa, his indignance in overdrive.

Pet ownership, what a pleasure, Daisy had thought as she

limped slowly back to the kitchen.

"So, he mainly only got to this side of the counter before he was run out the way he got in," Cluero said, sinking onto a kitchen chair that was thankfully free of debris, "unfortunately, that's where the knife drawer was, which was obviously his target anyway."

"I just don't know how he found out about his oversight and was tipped off to come and correct it," Daisy said, rubbing her temples in slow circles.

"Well, we have the DNA now thanks to your precocious pets, but I might have the answer to that question," Cluero said, looking directly at Sylvia who was typing away on her phone, "it seems that what's said in this room doesn't stay in this room, does it, Mrs. Carmichael?"

"Eh?" Sylvia looked up, but clearly hadn't been listening.

"I've done some searching, and it seems one of your book club ladies has criminal connections," Cluero said, one eyebrow raised as if questioning whether the housekeeper already knew this.

"Criminal connections?" Sylvia echoed back, though rather more subdued.

"Oh Lord," Daisy prayed aloud, "please no more revelations."

Unfortunately, it seemed today wasn't the day for the vicar's pleas to be granted.

12. FISH

"So you're telling me you ran a random search on Lillymouth residents with a criminal record and Charlie Buckley came up?" Sylvia looked pale without her usual make-up, and even paler since Detective Cluero had informed her that Maggie Buckley's ne'er-do-well son had set his mother's messaging account up so that he could see every one of her texts. Unbeknownst to either his mother or the book club ladies it seems Charlie Buckley was not only passing on this info, but he was also being instructed how to act upon it. By whom, now that was the real question. Cluero showed a mug shot photo to both women. It was the same guy who had posed as the curate, though without what had now obviously been a fake beard and glasses.

"Aye," Clero shook his head, "I put out a call to have him picked up and lo and behold there was a random cutlery drawer in the boot of his vehicle. I should think the DNA you have that the vet collected will be the definitive corroborating evidence putting him at the scene of the crime here. I've only spoken to the man briefly, and he's not keen to talk. Not that I'm surprised. Your pets did a good number on him, we had to have the station nurse have a look at his minor injuries, so you can imagine the mood Buckley was in by the time I got to him. But hopefully I can get it out of him who he's working for. He's a small fish in a big pond, mind you, probably quite a few people between him and the person who set you up, Vicar. Besides, I get the impression he'd prefer jail time to having to admit to the big boss that he's been caught. Quite a lot of fear behind his eyes."

"I'm so sorry, so sorry, stupid phone! I didn't even know Charlie was back in town. Maggie told him to sling his hook years ago after he stole her rainy day money," Sylvia slammed the offensive device down on the table and scrubbed at her face, "I thought I recognised something in the eyes of that supposed clergyman the other week, but I'm old, I've met so many people and seen so many TV shows. I hadn't seen Charlie since he was a teenager must be a decade ago now, so he wasn't even on my radar." The housekeeper looked tired and worn down, nothing like the woman who had moved into the vicarage all those months ago. Daisy felt completely responsible.

"It's not your fault, Sylvia. You're entitled to friends and an outlet just like the rest of us," Daisy limped around to put her arm around her housekeeper's shoulders.

"Aye, but maybe keep the details of the murder investigation to yourself from now on," Cluero added, "as it is, though, we've caught the man who stole the items which helped set up the vicar here, so that's a new lead and ultimately you've helped rather than hindered the case, Mrs. Carmichael. This time, that is. We might not be so lucky next time. I wouldn't want you in danger again like last night."

"No, no, I'll be moving back in," Daisy interjected quickly.

"Is that a good idea?" Cluero and Sylvia both asked.

"I could go and stay with Lydia Stanley," Sylvia added, "she has three cats of her own plus a miniature dachshund so I doubt adding more animals to the mix will make much difference. Hopefully she's got a bigger cat box I can borrow though."

Daisy doubted very much whether that would be a smooth amalgamation of fur and feathers, but didn't say so. She really wanted to stay at the florist's with Gerald, so eagerly accepted her housekeeper's offer, "I'll ask Joe to help you move your things, along with the bird cage and such."

"Right well, if that's all decided, I'll see what I can get out of Buckley and I'll report to DCI Ornsley on the introduction of reasonable doubt into your case, Vicar, now that we can prove the items used in the murder were indeed stolen from the vicarage. In the meantime, you two stay out of trouble," Cluero gave them both a stern glare before smiling gently to soften it.

Knowing as she did that Bunch was currently holed up in her vicarage bedroom covered in someone else's blood, Daisy was pretty sure trouble had already been found, but she smiled at the detective and mumbled what she hoped were suitably reassuring promises. The line between truth and dishonesty, between reality and nightmare had become so blurred for the vicar in recent times, that she hoped God would see her heart and understand. *Maybe even strike down the person who caused all of this in the first place… was it wrong for a woman of God to want that?*

"Now, before you get angry, hear me out," Gerald sat on the edge of Daisy's bed in the vicarage, his elbows on his knees as he leant forward with his head in his bony hands.

Daisy let out a long sigh and sat down beside him, rubbing the florist's back in slow circles the way he had for her so many times before, "I'm not angry, Gerald, I'm worried. I know you'd do anything to help me clear my name. Please tell me you didn't kill anyone."

He turned sideways to look directly at her, his expression softening as Daisy gave what she hoped was a reassuring smile, "No, love, I didn't kill him. That's not to say I didn't want to. But to be honest I'm not actually sure what good I did because all the threats of violence and actual bodily harm won't seem to make the man retract his statement."

Daisy's head throbbed and she knocked back some painkillers with a glass of tepid water that had been standing on her bedside table for goodness knows how long. She simply didn't have the energy to get up. That done, she moved so that she was sitting with her back against the headboard and encouraged Bunch to do the same, resting her head on his shoulder and holding the hand that still displayed the remnants of his bloody encounter.

"We'll have to make this explanation quick, because I need to help Sylvia clear up the boot room and kitchen," Daisy gave a brief description of the events of that night and morning.

"So, if that casts reasonable doubt on your part in the murder, can they rescind the arrest?" Bunch's large eyes looked so hopeful Daisy felt awful being the bearer of more bad tidings.

"No, sweetheart, no, that'll still be for the court to decide. Only proving my innocence will get the charges dropped. And to do that we'd need to know who the real culprit was," Daisy rubbed her thumb around his palm finding that the motion soothed her too.

"Well, that's what I was trying to do today, really I was, love. After Cluero dropped that hint that Briggs may be behind the false witness statement I went up there and challenged the man on it. He wouldn't admit why he did it but didn't bother to deny it either, just said his hatred for you is well known, but I'm sure someone put the little weasel up to it. Bribed him maybe. But no amount of threats or violence would make him tell me. He says there are bigger men than me to be afraid of. I think I broke his nose though, so I guess that's some satisfaction."

"Gerald! You can't be getting yourself locked up for assault. I bet the first thing he did when you left was report you to the police."

"Somehow, I doubt that. The man looked ill with worry, Daisy, he didn't even bother to bluster and blame, to threaten me with arrest in his usual style. He looked defeated. I think he may have well bitten off more than he can chew this time. He's used to being a big fish but I think he may've encountered a shark."

"Funny, Cluero was talking in ocean metaphors too," Daisy mused, "saying Buckley was a small fish. And here you are saying Briggs is a bigger fish, but not the top of the food chain. Who is though? Who could make Briggs give a false statement and then leave him too frightened to rescind it. I mean, do you even think the man will be able to testify in court?"

"Not in his current nervous state, I'd doubt it. Which of course won't make the one responsible for all this any happier, though maybe seeing their plan falling apart will make them do something rash to out themselves," Bunch kissed the top of her head gently.

"Well, no more threats and violence from you, please,

there's more than one way to skin a cat, and I've just had an idea of how we can get solid proof of Briggs' dishonest involvement," Daisy said, sitting up quickly, "unfortunately, it involves Violet Glendinning."

13. TWO BIRDS, ONE STONE

The afternoon had been spent sorting out the mess in the vicarage and helping Sylvia move the animals. Thankfully, Joe had done most of the driving to and fro, leaving Daisy and Bunch to pack a few more of her own things from the vicarage. By the evening, the pair were exhausted and sat cuddled up together on the sofa in the flat above the florist's, pretending to watch a show about doing up your house on a budget. Joe had kindly asked them to go for dinner at The Boatyard the following evening and Daisy hoped that by then her own investigations might be slightly further forward. The day had presented no time to speak to Violet so that would have to wait till the morning, though recent events had solidified in Daisy a new confidence, a restored desire to clear her name and to stand up for herself. Where before there had seemed no hope with a case against her that was apparently watertight, now Daisy could see the cracks forming, the light forcing its way through, and she intended to use this to her full advantage. No more hiding. No more apologetically removing herself from town life in case she made others feel uncomfortable. Reverend Daisy was on a mission.

They must've both dozed off in front of the tele, as Daisy only became aware of the hammering on the shop window downstairs at the same time as her mobile phone began to ring.

"It's Cluero," she answered the call as Bunch dragged himself down the narrow staircase to let the man in.

"Sorry, Detective, he's coming down now," Daisy yawned around the words as she hung up.

"Apologies for calling round so late," the Welshman said as he followed Bunch up into the flat, "there's been a development and I didn't want to discuss it over the phone."

"Oh?" Daisy was wide awake at hearing that.

"Yes, unfortunately by the time I got back to the station

earlier to interview Mr. Buckley again, he had apparently already been released without charge. Not only that, but the DNA evidence was seemingly lost on its way to the lab," the expression on Cluero's face said everything Daisy needed to know about his views on that.

"How? The evidence was all there, the drawer, the fingerprints, the hairs and everything. How could he be let off without so much as a proper interrogation?" Daisy's voice was high pitched as she began pacing the room.

"I wondered that myself, believe you me. I checked the computer and it seems DCI Ornsley himself questioned the man then deemed there was no case to answer to."

"That can't be right, surely?" Bunch's forehead was a maze of worry lines, deep troughs which Daisy wished she could smooth out with her fingers.

"No, it can't. There's something fishy going on, internally I mean. I need to do some investigating of my own, but it's difficult to know who to trust even within my own team any more. I know you and Matlock never saw eye to eye, Vicar, but you were actually both quite similar in that you see justice as a black and white concept. People must be held accountable for their actions, that's what Matlock believed. If she'd come across anything suspicious on the job she wouldn't let it lie, even if it was a colleague who was into some shady dealings. Now I wonder if she was onto something and someone inside needed to get rid of her. By framing you for her murder, they would've killed two birds with one stone."

"Oh my goodness!" Daisy exclaimed, "Do you mean Ornsley could be crooked? I mean, I told him about the potential fingerprints, so maybe it wasn't Sylvia leaking information that caused Buckley to break in when he did. After all, your boss didn't arrange the forensics officer did he? You had to do that. But why me? I've never met Ornsley before my interrogation for murder. Why would he want to set me up? What does he have against me? How would he even know about the childhood bullying that apparently provided the perfect motive for me to murder Michelle?" Bunch brought Daisy gently into his embrace as her heart felt like it might burst out of her chest. It seemed that for every answer, there were five more questions jumping in to replace it and taking up valuable headspace.

"I need to look into it, Daisy, but in the meantime, say nothing to anyone. What I've shared with you both must remain in this room. These are some serious allegations we're talking about and I need time to get the full picture. I could be wrong, but rest assured I'll find the truth either way."

"Please don't put yourself in danger, Detective, if they could get to Matlock without shining any light on their own nefarious activity, blaming it all on the local vicar in fact, then no one's safe…" Daisy let the words hang between them as all three stood in the middle of the tiny room. If only she knew who 'they' were.

Cluero merely smiled and shook his head, raised his hand in a silent wave and headed back downstairs, leaving Daisy on legs that felt like jelly.

"Wait here love while I lock the door and then we'll talk," Bunch said, with Daisy feeling the chill as he moved away.

"I just don't understand it," Daisy said, her body trembling despite Gerald's arms around her and a blanket over them both. The television still droned on in the background, with neither having bothered to turn it off. The constant noise was better than an ominous silence, that's for sure.

"Neither do I, love, neither do I, there just seem to be so many threads, so many pieces of the puzzle, and yet I get the impression it's the biggest piece of all that we're missing. Once we have that, we'll hopefully see where you fit into the grander picture. One thing's for sure, though, I'm not letting you out of my sight until this is all resolved. The more of their scheming that's exposed, the more desperate the true perpetrator may get and I can't lose you, Daisy, not now, not ever."

For once, the vicar didn't protest. Independence and self-sufficiency was one thing, living under the Lord's wing was another, but right now she needed someone of blood and bones to share the burden. At last, Daisy realised there was no shame in that. It wasn't a weak versus strong situation, either. She could be strong and still accept support. She could be Daisy Bloom and ask for help.

It was a revelation indeed.

14. A PENNY FOR THEM

Despite his protestations that she should not go alone, Daisy had explained to Gerald several times that Violet would respond best if it were just the two women in earshot of the delicate conversation she intended to initiate. The vicar wanted to speak to the head of the parish council alone and hopefully catch the other woman off guard. As a compromise, though, she let him accompany her as far as the main town square, where Violet Glendinning's home was one of the pretentious town houses on The Parade. Despite the sea breeze and the fact that she was dressed only in a sundress, Daisy felt the sweat dripping down her back as they walked down Cobble Wynd, Bunch on one arm and her stick in the other. The knowledge that what she was about to do wasn't strictly legal had triggered her anxiety, but was not enough to deter Daisy from going through with it. What did legality matter when you were a suspected murderer anyway?

A cheerful, "See you later, Vicar!" from Stan Barnes who was outside cleaning the bakery front window was quickly shushed by his wife, Cathy, but Daisy thought no more on it, simply happy to receive a friendly greeting. She would certainly miss being the vicar here, despite the town's negative associations in her own past and also with her current precarious position. She had always loved Lillymouth's position between the moors and the sea, the long history of the town and its community spirit. Even if she managed to come out of this whole nightmare unscathed, however, Daisy wasn't sure if she would take up the role of parish incumbent again. After all, where had been the support from the Christian church in all of this? Where had been the love of Christ or the reassurance of justice in her treatment by her superiors in the institution? Goodness me, they hadn't even asked her version of events let alone believed her. It had left Daisy with a heavy heart and a lot to dwell upon – much of which would have to wait for now.

"A penny for them," Bunch whispered.

"Oh, my thoughts aren't worth that much," Daisy replied, smiling up at him wanly, "I was just thinking of the future."

"In what way, love?"

"Well, whether I have one for a start, and after that? Who knows. I thought I was called to be God's mouthpiece within the community, and I haven't lost faith in Him, rather in those who also work for him, if that makes sense."

"Well, if you're talking about being left high and dry by the bishop, then it makes total sense. I know your ultimate boss is God, but with all those human frailties in between you and Him, the power struggles you're caught up in and the hierarchy you have to adhere to in your vocation… Let's say, I can certainly understand your doubts on that score. Be a florist, it's much simpler," he shot her a wink as they arrived at the bottom corner of Cobble Wynd, "go on, you do what you need to and I'll meet you right here when you're finished." Bunch had chosen a spot where he could see Daisy every step of the way to her destination and back again.

"Thanks, I doubt I'll be long before I'm given my marching orders. Ten minutes tops."

Daisy had been correct. In fact, it was less than eight minutes before she was back with Bunch again. Her task was complete, however, so in that sense time taken was meaningless.

"Did she agree?" Bunch asked as they strolled down towards the promenade arm in arm.

"Reluctantly. Very reluctantly, as you can imagine, but yes. She'll ask Percy to check Briggs' bank account and see if he's had any unusual deposits or withdrawals in the past couple of months. I mean, the man shares private details of everyone else's finances with her, so I doubt he'll have any qualms. Such a ridiculous character to have as the town's only bank manager."

"What did you have to blackmail her with?" Bunch whispered.

"Tsk, tsk, sweetheart, such a dirty word," Daisy flashed a small grin, "I simply reminded Mrs. Glendinning of the favour she owed me since I helped her out when she was accused of Jugger's murder."

"Well, you did help her out, but only by proving it was her son and his lover," Bunch raised a cheeky eyebrow eliciting another grin from the vicar.

"I may have also mentioned that I was sure the

financial ombudsman would be grateful to hear about Percy's indiscretions," Daisy felt herself blushing from the memory of her own audacity. Anyway, needs must, and it had worked. Violet should have the details in the next day or two and Percy would no doubt be none the wiser that he'd been pumped for information since he was used to his wife's nosiness. This meant that Daisy might have a name to work with if Briggs had indeed been bribed to either give the witness statement or to keep quiet since doing so. And that would be progress, which is what she needed.

"I'm proud of you, love," Bunch whispered and bent down to kiss the vicar, right there in the middle of the street.

"Thank you," Daisy replied, accepting the affection and not caring who might be watching. She'd spent too long worrying what other people thought. It was time for Daisy Bloom to live a little.

Daisy and Bunch turned up just before six, per Joe's instruction, slightly confused when they couldn't get parked outside the little coffee shop which was attached to his house. Daisy didn't suspect anything, though, not even when she read the handmade banner above the door which said 'Are Vicker is not Gilty!' In fact, it was only when the lights flicked on and everyone shouted "Surprise!" that the vicar realised this wasn't to be the quiet meal she'd thought. Instead, the room was filled with many of her parishioners – from the Sunday school children who'd made the sign, to Gemma, Paul, and Billy from the local pub. Of course, Stan's comment from that morning now made sense, as did Cathy's telling him to be quiet, as the whole thing had been kept a secret. Organised by Joe and Sylvia, almost everyone Daisy knew had come out to show their support for the vicar in her time of need.

Daisy was at once choked with emotion and equally horrified. Forced to be centre of attention, when her innocence wasn't even ascertained yet… well, if the ground would have opened up and another treasure tunnel appeared right then and there, Daisy would have happily escaped through it. Gerald, too, seemed highly uncomfortable with all the attention and disappeared quickly to the side as Daisy was swamped with hugs and voices of support.

"Ah, thank you," Daisy tried to speak up over the din, sending an 'I'll speak with you later' look to Joe and Sylvia who both appeared very pleased with themselves. From the ladies' book club – certain of whom refused to catch Daisy's eye due to recent developments – to the journalling for wellness group, the shopkeepers to the local policeman and his wife, only a few notable faces were missing.

"We're all here for you, Daisy," Bea had waited at the back of the crowd and now managed to reach her friend and give her a big hug.

"And where's my little namesake?" Daisy asked, scanning the room and seeing Bea's husband, Andrew, but not their daughter.

"Mum's babysitting, but that reminds me actually, Dad's getting a long service award from the force at an awards ceremony on Tuesday night and we were wondering if you could watch little Daisy Mae in the Book Nook for us so we could all be there for him. Bring your boyfriend if you like!"

Daisy blushed hotly at the teasing, shot a quick look at Bunch who was like a fish out of water, and immediately agreed. Any time spent with the toddler was precious indeed.

The show of support, the food that everyone had made at home and brought to share, the words of appreciation for what she did as vicar in the parish, it was all lovely. Lovely and a bit too much. After less than an hour, Daisy found herself making excuses for them both so that she and Bunch could escape into the fresh air. Guilt assailed her as she felt like she was running out of her own party, thrown by people who loved her and cared about her wellbeing, when Daisy herself didn't know if she even wanted to be their vicar any more. And that was all before you considered the possibility of prison.

No, it was well meant but just too much.

15. DON'T LOOK BACK

The journey back in the car should've taken less than five minutes, especially since a lot of the townsfolk were still down at The Boatyard meaning Lillymouth's roads were very quiet, but a couple of minutes in Bunch took a sharp right and steered them back towards the coastal road.

"That car behind's been following us since we turned off the promenade," he said, glancing in his rearview mirror, "don't look."

Daisy tried to inconspicuously see in the passenger side mirror but could only make out the harsh glare of headlights. When the car behind them also made the same turn, effectively taking them in a big circle back almost to where they'd begun, Daisy knew they were being deliberately followed.

"Who do you think it is?" She asked, her voice shaking to match her hands.

"Now that's the question. No one with any good intentions, I'd say," Gerald sped up. He had two options. Either continue this way and come into Lillymouth at the top end of the town, then try to fiddle through the small streets and lose their pursuer before they reached home, or park up in the coastal car park which sat in the sand dunes behind the caves and try to outrun them to reach the tunnels under the town. Of course, he had to take into account Daisy's disability and the fact that there may be more than one would-be assailant in the car behind them.

"Listen love, I'm going to lead them a merry dance down the coast here and back, but I need you to prepare yourself."

"Prepare myself?" Daisy hated the wobble in her voice.

"Yes love, when I park up, the moment the car comes to a standstill, you get out and start running. Go down the steps and through the underpass that runs under the dunes, then cut left and into the caves. You know where the tunnel entrance is from the other night, don't you? The tide looks fine from here."

"Gerald, I don't know if I ca…"

"You can, love, and don't wait for me, you hear? Don't look back, just run."

"No! You have to come too, I'm not leaving you…"

"You must and you are, love, I'll be behind you, I promise. Just get as far up the tunnel as you can under your own steam and then I'll be there to help you move the plyboard at the other end under the shop. Nothing to worry about."

"Nothing to worry about? Gerald, are you mad?"

The car behind was getting gradually closer, the driver's confidence growing with the lack of other road users the further they got out of town.

"Sorry, love, they're getting impatient, I'm spinning a U-turn and heading back. I'll swing off the road into the car park as sharply as possible hoping they sail right on past and have to reverse. That'll buy you some time. I'll deal with the rest. I love you."

It was the first time he'd said the actual words and not just intimated them by calling her 'love' or by his actions which spoke it so loudly, and Daisy wanted to cry out with the unfairness of it all.

"I love you too, Marcus," she kissed him on the cheek, then gathered her walking stick in her hands and prepared to run for her life.

It took Daisy a long while to reach the shop through the tunnel, stopping as she did every few metres to rest her leg, to turn on Bunch's permanent battery-powered lights that were dotted along the route, and to listen carefully for any sign of the man himself. Nothing but her own breathing and the squeaking of furry residents reached her ears and Daisy felt the wet, silent drops of her tears as they ran down her cheeks and dripped off her chin.

She had reached the last bulb and knew the entrance to the florist's basement must be just up ahead on the left. How she would move aside the large piece of plywood which kept the hole boarded up Daisy had no idea, and somehow that seemed the last of her worries. For if Marcus Caldwell was not here to see it through with her – this absurd nightmare, this mad adventure of life – then what was even the point? Daisy reached under the collar of her cardigan for the small cross which hung there and fingered it gently, not formulating a prayer intentionally just letting the words roll through her head, knowing God would hear her.

Apparently today was the day for Daisy's pleas to be answered.

Thank you, Jesus, Daisy's heart leapt with gratitude when several minutes later – she'd completely lost track of time at that point – footsteps could be heard making their way closer to her through the tunnel. Now, maybe it was Daisy's innate hope or belief, her strong faith or the fact that she simply felt attuned to him, but she didn't for once contemplate that this would be any other than her florist.

Thankfully, there was no need to face the worst as it was indeed Marcus Caldwell who appeared out of the dank gloom. Not Gerald Bunch, a simpering florist who couldn't say boo to a goose. No, this was Caldwell, a strong, brave man who had stood up to his love's tormentor and won – or to one of them, at least.

"Who was it?" Daisy asked as Caldwell stepped quickly past her to move the barrier and let them into the basement before making sure it was securely put back in place.

"Let's get upstairs, love, I need to catch my breath a moment."

It was only when they were in the harsh glare of the display lights in the shop that Daisy really saw the man who had come back to her. Bent in pain and clutching his right side, Marcus was once again bloodied and this time bruised too, his right eye already swollen and bloodshot and his cheekbone puffy.

"My goodness! Who did this to you?" Daisy asked again as Caldwell turned off the lights plunging them into darkness for a second as he opened the door to the stairway, "Let's get a doctor, get you to the hospital or something. Oh, but the car is back at the beach and mine is on Church Street…"

"Shh love, nothing to panic about. I'm here, likely just a bruised rib and a black eye. I've had much worse back in boarding school," he deliberately turned on just the table lamp in the flat and sank down onto the settee.

Daisy joined him, quickly taking the man's hand and ignoring her own pain. What a pair they made, "Tell me, please."

"It was that guy, Buckley I think, since judging by the state of his face someone had already had a good go at him before me. His boss mustn't have been too happy he got himself arrested. Obviously acting on orders again tonight, but thankfully alone."

"Did you get it out of him? Who he's working for?"

"No love, all he said was that you need to stop meddling in your own murder case. What a load of rot! His job was just to frighten us, I think, but believe me it didn't work, just made me angry. I gave as good as I got, made sure he wouldn't be following me until I was safe in the tunnel and out of range. I did leave a message with him, though, for his boss. A verbal promise to the one who's putting you through all this."

"What was that?" Daisy's first thought was to hope he hadn't made matters worse. Though how they could be worse, she wasn't sure.

"That I'm waiting for him. This big guy they're all afraid of. I'm waiting here for him and he'll have to go through me to get to you, Daisy love."

Daisy heard her own sharp intake of breath, felt sick at the implication of what Marcus had said and ran her clammy hands over her skirt in absentminded agitation. She was too shocked to cry, too scared to move, there was only one thing Reverend Daisy Bloom could do.

Pray.

16. MILK DRUNK

No doubt Daisy's nemesis had been angered by Caldwell's threat, but would he have been needled enough to make a move himself? To come out of the darkness into the light? Daisy had thought on that into the early hours whilst Marcus himself didn't seem to care that the threat against them was heightened, or at least certainly didn't show any fear in front of Daisy. They had snuggled together in his bed after both had showered off the remains of the day – mainly because neither was prepared to let the other out of their sight – and Caldwell had appeared to sleep well, whereas Daisy had tossed and turned partly due to pain, partly due to worry.

She needn't have been so acutely distressed, however, as that next day absolutely nothing of note happened. Marcus had thought it best not to tell Cluero about the chase, since doing so would perhaps put that detective in further danger himself. So, to all intents and purposes life went on as if the whole evening ordeal had never happened. Marcus' injuries aside, there was no evidence otherwise. Daisy certainly preferred to think it had been nothing more than another of her nightmares, and so threw herself into making life seem as 'normal' as possible. Marcus seemed to understand her unspoken decision and so the two of them worked alongside one another in cosy harmony in the small florist shop which had been neglected recently. It all came back to Daisy quickly, the cutting of stems, removing excess foliage, arranging bouquets – things she had always found therapeutic in her youth.

Locals, happy to see the small shop open again and keen to support their own, popped in for a chat and to discuss arrangements for upcoming birthdays and wedding anniversaries, tactfully refraining from commenting on the florist's black eye. Marcus said his order book had rarely been as full nor his little floristry so busy and said it must be down to his beautiful new co-worker. Daisy had blushed, easily falling back into the simple life she had shared with her grandmother when green fingers and late night hot chocolate had been her refuge from a school life where Daisy had never fit in. Of course, a large cause of that had been Michelle Matlock and her friends, but even without their bullying Daisy had always felt different. So too in the clergy, her voice had been lost amongst those happier to conform, to not ask quite so many questions of the status quo.

Yet here, here she finally felt at peace. She had come full circle – well, almost, anyway. Daisy had seen too much of humanity, faced too much, endured too much, lost too much to ever be the little girl she once was. But that girl was still inside her, still reaching for the light, not all hope extinguished. Not yet at least.

Tuesday arrived and by now Daisy was getting antsy. Seeing danger around every corner, expecting it even, she was constantly on edge. Neither Caldwell's unwavering reassurance, nor Joe's twice-daily calls, not even Sylvia's updates on the animals' antics could distract Daisy from the fact that nothing bad had happened for the past four days. What was coming was inevitable, she felt it in her chest, and the prolonged anticipation was starting to take its effect on the vicar. She had heard nothing from Violet, nothing from Cluero either, and Daisy had tried to be patient. To be thankful for the quiet normality. Really she had. But it had to end – Daisy never once doubted that she was now living on borrowed time, that her beautiful life on Cobble Wynd with Marcus could only ever be temporary – and in that sense, Daisy would prefer it to be sooner rather than later.

Well, we really must be careful what we wish for…

Marcus was in the kitchen making them a summer prawn salad for tea when the call came. Seeing it was Bea, Daisy had no qualms about answering, having not spoken to her friend since the surprise party on Friday night.

"Daisy! Are you running late? We need to get going or we'll miss the awards ceremony. We have to get to Whitby for it," Bea sounded exasperated and Daisy tried to flick through her recent memories to find the cause. It had been a bad pain day though, her rising stress levels having a physical effect on her, and so the vicar's brain was foggy with medication and tiredness.

"Ah, awards?"

"My dad's long service medal. Can you still babysit?"

"Oh! Yes, of course, we were just on our way," Daisy fibbed, waggling her finger in the air to get Caldwell's attention and rushing into her room to find her shoes, "we'll be there in five."

It was a mad dash down Cobble Wynd, which saw Daisy trip more than once saved only by Marcus' grasp on her arm. Nevertheless, they arrived just six minutes later, breathless and windswept, but they were there.

"Thank you, really, we appreciate it," Bea and Andrew were out the door and on their way like ships passing Daisy in the night, leaving her with a sleepy toddler and no time for instructions on what to do with her.

"Not to worry," Marcus said, "we needn't go up to the flat, we'll just stay in the Book Nook here, lock the front door and read her stories on the sofa, then we can snuggle her while she sleeps. No fuss, not a problem. Andrew said they'd only be a couple of hours so we can manage that, can't we?" His completely uncertain expression made liars of his confident words as the man looked to Daisy for reassurance.

"Um, yes, yes, there's a bottle here on the coffee station with milk in it I think, and there are cuddly toys in her playpen there so… Oh!" It turned out that little Daisy Mae had rarely been left with anyone other than her grandmother, Morag, certainly not with her mother and father out of sight, and she wasn't too happy with the situation. The crying began softly and within seconds had reached ear-splitting proportions. The couple could barely think let alone hear each other and so Operation Distract the Baby began.

It was no surprise then, that Daisy missed the text message from Violet detailing what Percy had told her about Briggs' bank account. Nor that she missed no less than three calls from Cluero. The phone in her handbag didn't even see the light of day for the next hour and a half, until Daisy Mae had finally tired both herself and her babysitters out. Milk drunk and exhausted from screaming, the toddler finally fell asleep across Caldwell's chest, with the man himself looking as if he might join her at any minute.

Daisy tiptoed to the front counter of the shop where she had dumped her backpack when they arrived and pulled out the cheap, replacement handset that she was still using. With no salary payment coming, it was likely she'd be making use of this phone for the foreseeable future too. Stifling her gasp with her hand when she saw the attempted contact that she had missed, the vicar first opened the text message from Violet Glendinning. Unsurprisingly terse and to the point, she confirmed that yes, Briggs had received a large sum into his main umbrella account, though this was swiftly dispersed to his ancillary investments. Daisy could hear Percy speaking the words as she read them, as if Violet had taken down the message like a dictation. The deposit had been tracked to source and the name on the originating account was…

"It can't be!" Daisy felt her knees buckle and clung to the antique Victorian, wooden desk for support as her world crashed down around her.

17. IN ONE EAR AND OUT THE OTHER

Unable to move due to the toddler-sized weight pinning him down and reluctant to wake the child to begin round two, Caldwell motioned for Daisy to come back to the coffee nook at the back of the deep, narrow shop. Forcing herself forward on legs that felt almost weightless, clinging to the shelves along the side wall for support since her stick was on the floor beside the florist, Daisy made her way slowly towards him, her head reeling.

"What is it love? What's happened now?" Marcus asked in a strained whisper.

"I, ah, I got a text… from Violet. It confirms Briggs did

receive a random, significant payment earlier this month."

"And? Who was it from?"

Daisy could barely bring herself to look at the name on the screen, let alone to say it out loud, "Abigail, it was from Abigail Harper."

"Do you know an Abigail?"

"It's Bea, that's her full name, and Harper was her maiden name."

"My word, Daisy, what does that mean? Was she..?"

A soft tapping on the front door of the shop caught their attention and the smiling faces of Bea and Andrew could be seen with hands raised and waving at them through the glass. Daisy thought she might be sick.

"Here, take Daisy Mae and sit down, love, I'll let them in. Don't say anything, though, we need time to ah, get our heads round this."

Caldwell's recommendation of restraint went in one ear and out the other, however, as Daisy felt so betrayed, so beyond hurt that it bubbled out of her the moment Bea was close enough for a conversation.

"All okay? She settle quickly?" Andrew asked, unaware of the tension in the room.

Bea studied Daisy's face quietly, "Is it okay, Daisy? You seem upset."

"I am upset actually," Daisy blurted out, and not even Marcus' cautionary hand on her arm could stop her, "I'd like to know, really like to know, why you paid Robert Briggs to give a false witness statement. To swear that he saw me killing Michelle Matlock."

"What?" Bea sank down onto the opposite sofa while her husband quickly took their daughter from Daisy.

"Briggs. He was paid a large sum. Either to bribe him to speak up in the first place, or to stick with his story afterwards. Maybe he got cold feet. Is that what happened, Bea?"

"I don't know what you're talking about, Daisy. How long has she been acting like this, Bunch? Is she having a mental breakdown?"

"I, ah," Marcus tried to answer, but Daisy spoke over him.

"No, I'm in perfectly sound mind, and I'm sure the police can get the bank statements to prove what I'm saying."

"I just don't understand," Bea began crying.

"Right, that's enough," Andrew spoke up as Daisy Mae awoke and reached immediately for her mother, "you two had better get going."

Daisy ignored him too, "It was your name, Bea, or rather your name as was, Abigail Harper, on the bank statement. Were you even at an awards ceremony tonight or was that a ruse to get me here? What's the plan now, Bea?"

"A ruse, what the hell are you talking about? We trusted you, Daisy, left our precious Daisy Mae with you, have had your back despite what people are saying, and you repay us with what? Lies and accusations." Andrew was angry now, fishing his phone out of the inside pocket of his smart blazer and tapping through to his photographs from the evening, "Look, right here on the stage, there's Bea's dad Daniel Harper, with the two blokes he joined the force with forty years ago! Of course we were where we said we'd be."

Bea didn't give the phone that was thrust under her face more than a passing glance but something about it caught Caldwell's eye and he took the device straight out of Andrew's hand without asking. His eyes darkened with anger, his lips pursed tightly.

"Look love, look here, beside Harper, do you recognise him?"

"What? Oh!" Daisy took the phone herself and made sure that yes, she did recognise the man who had started working as a new cadet on the police force decades ago, alongside Bea's dad. Best buddies, brothers in arms, no other than DCI Richard Ornsley.

It was all too much, too confusing. Caldwell had searched Ornsley up online when it had come to light that the man had buried Daisy's request for fingerprinting in the vicarage, so he had an idea what the guy looked like despite never having met him in person. Daisy, of course, recognised the man who had interrogated her on a murder charge immediately. She felt sick to her stomach.

"This is the last time I'll ask," Daisy whispered, her eyes pleading to her erstwhile best friend – Daisy doubted they'd be friends again after this, "please Bea, tell me the truth, do you know anything about any money paid to Briggs? Do you know anything about who or why I was set up for murder?"

"No and no!" Bea bit the words out in an enraged whisper over the top of her daughter's head, "Now get out!"

Caldwell helped Daisy out of the Book Nook and into the summer's evening, surprised to see that the sun hadn't yet set although it was a low orange ball in the sky over in the direction of the moors. It was almost shocking to the pair that the earth was still turning as normal despite everything seemingly having been tilted on its axis in their own world. They both took several deep breaths, as if the salty air could cleanse them of the accusations, of the betrayal. As it was, the vicar was now unsure as to who had betrayed whom – was it Bea who had committed the unthinkable, or Daisy for accusing her friend of it?

Someone had created this web of lies and intrigue and Daisy felt they were all well and truly stuck in the middle of it now. Forced by the machinations of someone hitherto unknown into a space that was getting smaller and smaller as more elements of their deceit emerged.

Did Daisy really believe that Bea could, if not as the instigator, then at least knowingly be part of a plan to ruin Daisy's life? The vicar of a year ago would have immediately known the answer, but since their fallout – which lasted for six months or so and saw Bea changing her mind about having Daisy as her daughter's godmother – she now found herself unsure in their relationship. Was the renewed friendship real or had it all been a ruse?

"Come on, love, we'll figure it all out at home," Marcus put his arm around Daisy's waist and helped her back up the cobbled street.

Whilst she admired his optimism, Daisy wasn't sure they would figure it all out as he'd said. From where she stood, the waters were becoming murkier rather than clearer, and with every new revelation Daisy's energy for sustaining the fight decreased.

18. NO LOVE LOST

As the couple walked up the almost-deserted street, all of the shops being closed for the evening, it was Caldwell who first spotted the figure standing outside the florist's, "Stay behind me, love."

"It looks like Cluero," Daisy squinted to make out the man's features.

"Well, no need to take any risks."

The vicar had been correct, though, and it was indeed the Welshman waiting for them to return, "Apologies for turning up uninvited yet again. I did try calling, Vicar, but when the fourth call went unanswered I thought I'd make sure you were okay."

"Thank you, Detective, that was very thoughtful," they waited while Caldwell unlocked the door and then all filed up to the flat above.

"Was there a specific reason for your calls?" Daisy asked, slumping down onto the sofa, kicking off her shoes and tucking her legs up under her. How she was still functioning even semi-competently she wasn't really sure.

"There was, and again this information is just between the three of us, for you to use as you will."

"Understood," Marcus joined Daisy on the sofa and took her hand in his, whilst Cluero sat on the chair opposite.

"I'm not sure I can take any more bad news tonight," Daisy leant her head against Caldwell's shoulder.

"Oh?" The Welshman's eyes were alert for new information.

Marcus described Briggs' apparent windfall and that the account it came from was in Bea's name, adding as an afterthought that they now knew Ornsley and Harper were buddies who went a long way back.

"Maybe DCI Ornsley is the one who has it in for me, and Harper is helping him cover his tracks?" Daisy wondered aloud, "It's fair to say there's been no love lost between me and Bea's dad over the years. But I have no idea as to what Ornsley's motive would be."

The detective had become even paler during their explanations, not saying a single word until Daisy stopped to take a shuddering breath, "Okay, then what I was calling to say might well shed some extra light on that. I've done some digging myself, nothing official mind you, and rest assured I didn't let anything on to Ornsley. So, Daisy, it would seem that your mother's hit and run case was investigated by none other than Daniel Harper himself, though of course he was a much lower ranking officer then. Besides that, though, which I found in an old work log – a huge document of who was looking into which case, hours spent and so on, spanning years – the file itself has been deleted from the system in its entirety. Scene notes, witness statements, all gone from the computerized search. Unless they were too far back to have been uploaded in the first place, that is."

"What does that mean? That Ornsley killed my mum? That Harper knew he did and was covering for his friend as he led the investigation? That Ornsley wasn't involved at all and he's just a red herring? Was it an accident that needed hushing up or something more sinister?" Daisy's head reeled.

"There's more, I'm afraid. This lack of electronic documentation led me to the old paper archives. I was sure the paperwork would be there, but again, no case file for the hit and run. Nothing at all, no hospital records, scene of the crime witness statements, not even a one-page outline of the incident. This led me to look for the file on your Gran's murder. I didn't want to chance looking this up on the computer system with the other case and have an automatic alert sent to anyone internal who might have a vested interest, so I also looked for this in the boxes of archives."

"Was it there?" Caldwell asked, "Did any details remain?"

"Not of the file itself, no, that too had been disappeared like the other, but I searched for the end of year stats round up. The report shows cases outstanding, and the murder is on there. Chief investigating officer, Daniel Harper."

"No," Daisy shook her head vehemently, "I don't remember him interviewing me, it was some woman with a social worker present."

"Aye well, likely he didn't want you to recognise him. Maybe he never disclosed the conflict of interests that he was a friend of the family as that would've had him taken off the case," Cluero said.

"I did try to do this digging myself," Daisy began, "when I was a liaison officer in Leeds, but it always came up that I didn't have the right computer access."

"Hmm," was all Cluero replied.

"So, just to clarify," Caldwell's chin rested on steepled fingers, his expression above them intense, "Daniel Harper was the investigating police officer for both the death of Daisy's mum and for the murder of her grandmother some fifteen years later. A cynical person would say he insinuated himself into both of those cases to ensure the outcomes he wanted – namely that the culprit or culprits never be found and the investigations later dropped and eventually disappeared from the records altogether. After all, other than Daisy and Joe, I'd imagine there aren't many people left who would even remember let alone care enough to go digging. So, this raises the question of whether Harper was protecting himself or someone else. If the latter, then Ornsley is the obvious suspect."

"Quite so," Cluero's voice had the hint of a tremor as he replied, "both men in positions of power and almost impossible to make a case against, I would think. I've seen with my own eyes – or not, as is the case – that they can get rid of evidence as if it never even existed. They can hire men of dubious character like Buckley, plant evidence, change details on computerised statements, and bribe even influential men like Briggs. Blackmail perhaps. I'm so sorry, Daisy, I'm not sure where we go from here. I'm saddened to be working with such shady characters when we are meant to be protecting people and enforcing justice. If needed, I would testify in your defence, if they didn't get to me first..."

"Leave it with us," Caldwell spoke decisively, "anything you're party to from here on in could get you into hot water at work, or worse, place you in the firing line. Daisy and I will take care of it. We're so grateful for your help, Detective, thank you."

Cluero didn't look convinced. The Welshman's eyebrows were tightly drawn and the side of his mouth indented as if he were chewing on his gum, "I wouldn't advise doing anything... rash," was all he said before rising to leave.

On impulse, Daisy heaved herself up and hugged the man, who was clearly caught off guard.

"You, ah, take care of yourself, lass," he whispered, before following Caldwell downstairs.

Daisy couldn't sit back down. Her legs suddenly had too much energy, as if an electric pulse had been flicked on to flow through her limbs and torso. It was a nervous current which made her pace back and forth, wringing her hands together. Too het up to pray, too shocked to think clearly, one thing Daisy knew was that this was it. This was where it all ended, one way or another. The big reveal, the grand climax. An epic showdown. Whatever she and Marcus decided to do. But one thing she knew for certain – only the two of them would make this last stand. There were no other avenues of support to call on, nor would she put anyone else in potential danger.

This had always been her fight, and Daisy was ready for it to end.

19. BAIT

"No wonder Bea didn't want to ask her dad to look in the archives for me. How much do you think she knows?" Daisy asked Marcus as they snuggled back on the sofa together. He had both of her small hands nestled between his larger ones to stop them shaking.

"I'm not sure love, but to be honest I think that's low down on the list of things to think about. We need to flush the murderer out. Be it Ornsley or Harper, we need to force them to expose themselves so that we can see who exactly is at the top of this pyramid of lies. Then we need to deal with them."

Daisy didn't want to ask what Caldwell meant by that

last statement. Not yet anyway. Instead, she said, "So, how would we do that? Flush them out?"

"Well, I think we'll need to lead with our biggest advantage, the new information we have. Even embellish it a bit to make it seem like we know exactly who we're dealing with. Then we use the element of surprise to bring them down."

It was all rather vague for the vicar's liking, and no doubt extremely risky, "I don't want you in danger, Marcus."

"If you think I've come this far by your side just to hide now, then you're a silly bean," he replied, tilting Daisy's chin up with a long index finger and kissing her gently, "if anyone's staying out of the way then it's you, love, but until I hash out the details in my head I'm not sure how possible that will be. We may need to use you as ah, well, as bait."

"Bait?" Daisy gulped but straightened her back, "Whatever's necessary without getting anyone else involved."

"Very well, love, then leave the planning to me."

Daisy had a sense of finality, a foreboding if you will,

that saw her the next morning up with the lark and hurrying to The Boatyard to see Joe. Not to update him or anything like that, but rather to say her secret goodbyes somehow without the man knowing. For once, Marcus had let her drive the short distance by herself, leaving him deep in thought in the flat above the florist's shop. The man had barely slept, holed up in his room in focused concentration and surrounded by several sheets of paper covered in scribbles. Daisy had promised to be quick – just a flying visit to Joe and then one to Sylvia at Lydia Stanley's cottage on Fisherman's Row. Then back home. Caldwell had impressed upon the vicar the need for them to act quickly, lest their opponent strike the final blow before they had a chance to set things in motion on their own terms.

So, it would be fair to say that Daisy was a nervous wreck when she arrived at Joe's little lean-to cottage well before the coffee shop's opening time. All that was going on must surely have clouded the vicar's judgement if she thought the man who had known her almost all of her life wouldn't notice her clear agitation.

"Daisy, love, this is an early visit," the grey stubble was thick on the old fisherman's chin, his eyes bleary still, "is everything okay? Do I need to get my coat?"

"What? No, of course not, I just thought we could share a coffee, reminisce about Gran a bit. I had a dream about her last night," that was true at least, "about how you would row us across to Smugglers' Isle and leave parcels for the pirates. How we would dig about randomly looking for buried treasure and play hide and seek around the island. Gran was always relaxed on those days, as if we were in our own bubble." A stray tear made its way down Daisy's cheek.

"Aye lass, I remember those days well," the old man's own eyes had become glassy, "come in and we'll talk awhile."

There were tears shed, memories fondly recalled and even some laughter as Daisy and Joe reminisced on happier times. When it was time to leave they hugged each other tightly, no more words needed, and Daisy forced herself to not look back though the tears rolled down her face and her chest was tight with love for the man who had raised her as his own.

Arriving at the next destination on her whistlestop tour, the two visits couldn't have been more like chalk and cheese. The best word to describe the state of Lydia's cottage was bedlam. The mynah bird, it would seem, had formed an unlikely alliance with the miniature dachshund, in an effort to make a stand against the four cats. The house rabbit hated them all, and was intent on knocking over their food bowls, leaving small 'gifts' in their water troughs and generally making a nuisance of himself. Lydia seemed beside herself, the combined menageries of both houses having pushed her to the edge with their antics.

Of course, Daisy had forgotten that Sylvia was a late riser – no doubt because she spent half the night watching police chases – and so had to be summoned from her bed by Lydia, who took the opportunity to also shut Malone in the bedroom. It was an awkward five minutes as Lydia sat opposite Daisy at the tiny dining table, trying to make small talk that avoided awkward subjects and with Jacob claiming Daisy's lap as if he were laying a flag for his country on top of a hitherto unexplored mountain. The proud puss sitting up on his chunky rear thighs to make sure that all the other animals could see his lofty position, whilst secretly digging his claws in to avoid the vicar's efforts to de-throne him.

Finally, Sylvia emerged, hair in curlers, her nightdress crumpled and a rather angry looking rabbit in her arms. Cue hissing from Jacob, rabbit paws slapping the air ineffectually as Malone tried to struggle free of Sylvia's grasp and a general battle of wills, until Lydia gave Sylvia her seat at the two-person table and calm reigned for a precious few minutes.

"What is it petal? A development in the case? Have you been let off, your reputation restored as it should be?" Sylvia asked, thanking Lydia for the pot of tea and two china cups and saucers which appeared as if by magic on the table between them, followed swiftly by a toast rack accompanied by jams and butter. Lillymouth hospitality at its finest.

Daisy didn't have the stomach for food, but accepted the cup of breakfast blend and shook her head sadly, "No, no, I just thought I'd say hello."

"How many hellos have you been saying lass, if you don't mind me asking? Your face tells a story all of its own," the astute housekeeper asked.

"Ah, just a couple, just wanted to let you know I'm thinking of you, and we'll have you back in the vicarage as soon as possible. One way or the other."

"Now Daisy, don't you be thinking of doing anything rash. You know what your Gran would say, 'think first, act later,' and since she's not with us, I'm telling you instead. Don't do anything silly, Daisy. Leave it in God's hands."

Daisy nodded and forced a watery smile, unable to speak past the lump in her throat. If any divine intervention was planned, then she knew He would have to act quickly as time was running out on this mortal plane.

More words of wisdom from Sylvia, fewer and fewer responses from Daisy who was now fixated on what must come next, and the visit came to an end to the absolute infuriation of the vicarage cat. Jacob was vexed beyond belief to get his favourite bum cushion back – the vicar's lap – only to be indecorously removed some twenty minutes later as she said her goodbyes.

Nevertheless, leave she must.

The shops on Cobble Wynd were just starting to open as Daisy parked on Church Street and cut through to the florist's, her heart heavy and her feet heavier.

Today was the day.

20. DNA

"Sorry, love, I wasn't thinking clearly, I should've come with you," Marcus pulled Daisy into a tight hug the moment she appeared in the shop.

"No need, it was something I wanted to do alone anyway," Daisy sniffed and wrapped her arms around his waist.

"Right well, I have a plan. It's not foolproof, and it won't be pretty, but we need to move now before they do. Are you ready, Daisy?"

She had no idea whether she was prepared for what was to come or not, but the vicar nodded against his chest silently.

"Very well, then we'll begin with a phone call."

Daisy's hands shook as she dialled the direct number Ornsley had given her when she'd requested the fingerprint forensics. When he'd assured her she could rely on him directly for anything relating to the murder investigation.

"Detective Ornsley? Yes, it's Reverend Bloom here. I just wanted to let you know I've solved the case myself. I can prove not only my own innocence but exactly who the real murderer is... At the vicarage? No, I'm afraid my old injuries are playing up so I'm stuck here at the florist's until my mobility returns... Yes, it'll definitely have to be here for my statement, I'm afraid... Told anyone else? No, no, you said I should come to your directly... Yes, I won't leave, I'll wait here for your visit... Ah, I understand, yes, okay later today then. I'd rather not wait till this evening to be honest... Okay, thank you Detective, goodbye," Daisy turned to the side and violently threw up into an empty flower bucket. The sun shone through the wide windows of the florist shop, the scent of the blooms covering the smell of her sickly expulsion.

"And now we wait," Marcus said, pulling her to him.

"And now we wait."

The sun had long set and Daisy's body was stiff where she sat on the antique, highbacked wooden chair in the florist shop, positioned near the top of the stairs which led to the basement, just to the side of the rows of glass vases and only slightly back from the spot where her grandmother had been murdered. All lights were off to give the impression that the place was deserted and its inhabitants waited in the flat above. Daisy tried to force herself to stay awake, wriggling her fingers and toes in silent frustration, doubt seeping in as to whether this hours-long vigil had been in vain. Would someone even come today? And then, would it be the big boss or another lackey?

The sound of a scraping by the door to the shop brought the vicar out of her internal musings. They had closed up as normal, of course, not wanting to give any indication that all was not as it should be, trusting that whoever arrived would be able to pick an old and very simple lock. The chains and deadbolt had been left unsecured, so once past that small, metal deterrent the intruder would gain immediate access. She tapped the screen in her lap a few times before setting it in the shadows beside her.

Was Daisy surprised the visitor chose to break in

rather than announce their arrival like anyone else? Of course not, for this was surely her nemesis, the cause of all the grief and strife in Daisy's life and it was highly unlikely they would want to have a cosy, all-above-board chat about it all. Forcing herself to remain as still as a statue, Daisy waited with hitched breath to see who would emerge from the dark, cobbled street, where original streetlamps shed only small pools of an eery yellow glow around their perimeter. There was no such illumination near the florist shop, so its doorway remained in dark shadow.

The sound of metal scraping on metal, of clicks and shortly after of the latch being opened kept Daisy on high alert, until the door was pushed slowly open and a large figure filled the space. Forcing herself to breathe, Daisy waited until they had taken three steps into the room, closed the door quietly behind them and turned back towards her, before she flicked on the lights with the switch on the wall beside her, lighting up the whole shop with harsh illumination.

"Mr. Harper, I'd like to say this is a surprise, but it really isn't," Daisy forced her tone to remain even, her words paced as naturally as possible so as not to betray her true fear. There was a small satisfaction to be had, she had to admit, in the shock on the man's face, the small jerk of his head back towards the door as if he considered leaving or maybe to see if he'd been locked in.

"Reverend Daisy Bloom," the three words, spat out as if they were a blasphemy from a mouth distorted in disgust, were all he said, before advancing on the vicar.

"Stop right there," Daisy said it as authoritatively as possible, rising to a slow stand to face her adversary, "there is a lot to be said, is there not? You must surely have things you wish to explain to me? I know I have a lot of questions. We have both waited a long time for this day, haven't we?"

"You've always been a thorn in my side, haven't you? Even now, you won't die quietly, always had a mouth that was bigger than your brain," he paused, his head cocked to the side, eyes dark holes of anger, "Ornsley's a good right hand man but I needed to do this myself. One last time. I should've nipped the bud before it bloomed. If I'd known what a thorn in my side you'd be I would've."

Daisy forced herself to remain impervious to his taunts, "A thorn in your side? By being your daughter Bea's best friend?" She scoffed with a small, wry smile which Daisy knew would infuriate the man.

"I thought you had it all worked out, Daisy? Who

killed your mum – because yes, it was deliberate – and then your precious gran. Who set you up for Matlock's murder."

"I do, but I'd like to hear it from your side, you might as well brag a little about how you got away with it for thirty years," Daisy raised her eyebrows in silent invitation.

"Well, there you do have me, I mean it's something to be proud of, isn't it? Controlling investigations from the inside, pulling the wool over everyone's eyes. Your mother meant nothing to me. A fling, an unfulfilling little detour on the way home from work a few times. Nothing special. But then she was pregnant, and refused to get rid of it. Of course, with threats she kept quiet for the first couple of years, but then she started threatening to tell Morag, who'd had Abigail at about the same time as you were born. Wanted a piece of the family life I gave them, or at least the money to go out and find it. Blasted little blackmailer, got what was coming to her. If she'd died right there on the road it would've been better, but I had easy access to her in the hospital to finish her off there before she came out of the coma," he smiled widely. A grotesque grimace that had Daisy feeling like she needed to expel the meagre contents of her stomach once again. That, and finding out this monster was actually her own father. It was enough to fell her once and for all.

Nevertheless, she remain stoically calm, saying only, "As I suspected, go on."

"Well, then you and my gorgeous little girl befriended each other. I didn't see that coming, but it seemed harmless enough. I mean, I tried to bribe her to ditch you with toys and treats, attempted to get Morag to force the two of you apart but it was probably all too subtle. I couldn't risk my wife getting suspicious that anything was amiss, you see. Never mind, there was no link between you and I so I let it be. Until you came of age and started requesting your birth certificate – not that my name was on it, but I couldn't have you asking questions. Came here to tell your grandmother to make you stop and then one thing led to another. I hadn't planned that one, but even heat of the moment acts can be easily brushed under the carpet when you're the officer investigating them. It all had a silver lining, anyway, as you finally left the town, and good riddance I thought. A few blocks on the system to make sure you couldn't do any digging, to reject your application to be a police officer – you really didn't think you were up to that, did you? – and then getting a few buddies to keep eyes on you while you worked with those victims, easy-peasy. You really aren't the brightest."

"Well," Daisy said, having slowly edged to the side of the chair while the man was caught up in his boastful monologue so that she now stood behind it, "well, I suppose my DNA would be a match to yours, so there's that."

"Do you think I'm letting you out of here to get a DNA test?" He laughed, a harsh, bitter sound.

"Then there's the bank account which you stupidly put in your daughter's name. Been saving a little nest egg for her, have you? Shame you didn't offer to use it to help her when her business was failing earlier in the year and she was in a pit of despair."

"Why you..."

Daisy cut him off, "Well, you have to give me credit for something. A bit of forward planning and preparation of my own before you dispense of me like you did my mother and grandmother. Doesn't he, Bea?" Daisy lifted the electronic tablet that had been on the floor in the shadows beside her, the face of her former best friend coming into view on the face call as the pad came into the light, tears flowing from what she had just heard her own father admit to, "I guess we're sisters now."

"No!" The man's eyes bulged and he lurched forwards

to grab the device from her. Daisy gripped it tightly, tipping the chair into the murderer's path and racing down the stairs into the basement.

The heavy thud of the man's boots as he followed her came to an abrupt halt as he was struck on the back of the head by a small spade, his large body crumpling to the ground and plunging them into an almost unearthly silence, save from the sobbing of the woman in the Book Nook, who still hadn't disconnected the call.

21. THE APPLE OF MY EYE

"I'm so sorry Bea," Daisy whispered, before ending the call and making sure the sound recording that had been running in the background was saved to her device.

"I'm so proud of you, love," Marcus said, "Now we drag him through the tunnels to the beach and you decide what to do with him. It's your call, we can drown him or…"

"What?" Daisy asked. They hadn't discussed the plan beyond this point, her head unable to think past the confrontation. Only that she would lead the murderer to the basement where Caldwell would be waiting for him.

"Justice, love, that's what you wanted, isn't it? Well, how do you plan to get it through the judicial system? With him in such a high role, knowing the force protect their own. Do you really think Bea will testify against her dad? Let him live and he'll come up squeaky clean as per usual, there'll be no fair and unbiased investigation and our cards will be well and truly marked. Do you think he would give you the same compassion? He's already framed you for murder to cover for himself, no doubt because Matlock was onto him."

"We could lie and make him think Michelle posted me some evidence, or…" Daisy knew she was grasping at straws, "Anyway, that kind of justice… the kind you're talking about, that comes only from God. If we take it into our own hands, we're no better than Harper."

Caldwell bent down to tie the man's hands above his head with rope, his eyes still on Daisy as they continued their conversation and so was taken unawares when Harper headbutted him in the face. Daisy's father then took advantage of the man being dazed to get up from the floor and stagger towards her.

"Run!" Marcus shouted, sending Daisy into flight back up the stairs to the shop, Harper hot on her heels, as he himself went to grab the spade to follow them up.

Without her stick, Daisy tripped at the top and would've gone flying if not for a steadying arm that shot out, dragging her to the side and behind them.

A second after her, the vicar's grunting assailant, the man who was partly responsible for giving her life, emerged in the doorway only to be smashed over the head by a glass vase.

"That's for Wendy," Joe said, as the man crumpled to the floor in front of them, blood coming from his head, "and that's justice!"

Daisy allowed herself to be held by the man who was her true father, the one who had stood up for her through thick and thin and who had proven time and time again that he loved her unconditionally, whilst Marcus checked for a pulse.

"It's weak, but it's there. What shall I do?"

"Call an ambulance," Joe said, only a slight quiver in his voice to give any indication that he had just felled the man who had killed the love of his life, "if it's God's will, he'll live and we'll explain how it was self-defence. If he dies, so be it. He can face eternal judgement."

Daisy nodded her head, happy with the decision, and Marcus joined them in a brief group hug before making the call.

"How did you know?" Daisy whispered to Joe.

"Did you think you could fool me, lass? With a trip down memory lane and a pat on the back? Nay, I didn't know who or what, but I knew something was going down tonight. I just thought whoever it was would wait till at least midnight, not get here before ten. I would've been here sooner, but I went to visit your grandmother's grave and the minutes got away with me. Anyway, I made it in time. That's what matters."

"What matters is that you've always been there for me. Not just tonight, Joe," Daisy squeezed his arm and kissed his cheek gently, "thank you."

"You're my Daisy Bloom. My Viking Warrior Princess, of course I'll always be there for you. You're the daughter and granddaughter I never had and you were the apple of mine and your grandmother's eye, you know. Now I understand why Wendy was always afraid of that basta… of why she wouldn't tell me who he was. If only she had though, I could've…"

"Hush, there's no good can come of what ifs now."

Daisy sat back down heavily on the wooden chair, all fight suddenly gone out of her and her body limp with shock. She had the recording of Harper's confession and was sure Joe wouldn't go to jail for what he'd done. Safe in that knowledge, the vicar's mind and body shut down, lolling to the side in a dead faint.

22. A BUNCH OF BLOOMS

It was very strange to be on this side of the pulpit, to be standing at the top of the aisle beside the man who had just become her husband before God and with her back to all the assembled witnesses. Funnily enough, 'All Things Bright and Beautiful' didn't sound so gratingly shocking from down here, nor did Daisy feel any weight of judgement from the congregation. Partly because everyone was there to celebrate her wedding, and partly because she was no longer their parish vicar.

No, Daisy Bloom – or Caldwell as she now was – had happily been a florist for the past six months. Grateful to the new incumbent for taking over so smoothly and for conducting the marriage service now. They had even taken on all of the vicarage animals and the resident housekeeper with a benevolent grace, the likes of which Daisy knew she had never quite managed herself.

Joe had walked her up the aisle, her proud father, to Marcus who was patiently waiting to begin their new life together as man and wife. To have and to hold, to love and to cherish. As if he hadn't already saved her life on more than one occasion, he now wanted to be joined to her forever. Something that still made Daisy giddy with almost disbelieving happiness. Of course, their neighbours believed she had tamed the man of his brash buffoonery and odious, lecherous ways and that he'd only ever used the name Bunch as publicity for his floristry. Marcus' secrets were still safe.

The church had offered to welcome her back to its fold but she had declined. The former vicar still had her faith but didn't need a dog collar to feel she belonged. Faced with the decision to bloom where she'd been planted or to uproot and begin again, Daisy had of course chosen to remain with her handsome treasure hunter, in the full knowledge that their days would be anything but boring.

And perhaps, God willing, there would be a bunch of blooms after all.

Thank you so much for joining Daisy on her journey of discovery. There were more questions than even she realised, and the answers were certainly shocking, but she has her happy ending.

Perhaps Daisy's adventures are just beginning?

Look out for more from The Caldwell Chronicles in the future!

Have you visited Flora Miller, her feisty, feathered friend and the residents of Baker's Rise yet? If not, read on for an excerpt from the first book in the series, "Here Today, Scone Tomorrow."

23. EXCERPT FROM "HERE TODAY, SCONE TOMORROW – BAKER'S RISE MYSTERIES BOOK ONE"

Stan Houghton stormed out of the front door of the manor house known as 'The Rise' and strode off down the gravel driveway. His face, a molten red from his latest showdown with the 'lord of the manor' Harold Baker, contorted into a furious visage which matched his balled fists and heavy breathing. Surprised to see a familiar figure, dressed to the nines, approaching from the other direction, Stan tried to rein in his temper whilst making pleasantries.

"Good morning, Mrs. Edwards, fine day," he did not pause even for a second as they passed each other, nor did Stan listen for a reply as he hurried off back to the farm.

"If that's you again Houghton, you can get lost!" the shouted warning from indoors could be heard behind the flaking wooden main door of the manor, as its next visitor waited patiently on the doorstep.

"Oh, hello," his greeting was hardly welcoming even when Harold did pull the door open, "you'd better come in then!" He stalked into the main drawing room, eyeing his pet parrot suspiciously as if an outburst might ensue, and muttering, "not a word," as Harold waggled his finger in the direction of his feathered friend's perch.

The parrot, taking only one fleeting look at the outstretched finger, and choosing to also ignore the hastily given warning completely, screeched, "Old trout! Old trout!" and rose from his perch, flapping his wings viciously around the head of the woman who had just entered the room.

"Enough!" Harold said sternly, and the parrot finally decided to cease his assault.

"I gather this isn't a great time? I suppose Farmer Houghton was commenting on your latest rent increases for the village?" The woman tried surreptitiously to restore the elaborate up-do which the stupid parrot had managed to make look like a bird's nest. Giving up, she continued, "With the number of fields he has, I'd wager he's sorely affected." She stated it as a matter of fact, apparently unmoved by either the rent situation or the plight of a neighbour.

"Aye, well, he's always here threatening when the prices go up, but he pays it in the end. Just like they all do, if they want to keep living in Baker's Rise."

"Quite so. Anyhow, I've been baking and thought you might like a scone or two?"

Harold tried to hide his surprise. It was not a common occurrence for villagers to make their way up the hill for anything other than to air their gripes, let alone such a comely example of womanhood. For a moment, Harold was lost in sweet reminiscence of his many dalliances in years gone by. He was old now, stout in the waist and grizzly of feature, so he very much doubted that was what was on offer here. Nevertheless, he was intrigued as to what exactly would warrant such a special visit.

"Thank you kindly, dear lady, please take a seat and I will prepare a pot of tea," Harold licked his lips as he took in the sight of her, her face all made up to show her features at their best, her body encased in a tight tweed suit. When the lady didn't immediately sit, he was confused for a moment, until he realised that she would need to perch on top of one of the many mounds of paperwork, old magazines and newspapers which littered every available surface. Quickly, Harold swept a pile of brochures from the end of a settee and rushed off to the kitchen.

When he returned, the scones were arranged on one of the fine china plates, inherited from his mother, and which were stored in glass-fronted cabinets all around the room. Jam and butter – which she must have brought with her – sat in two dainty dishes complete with a miniature silver spoon and knife. Aye, she's after something, Harold thought to himself, his mind whirring with what he might get in return, as he set the tray on the small walnut coffee table between them, also cleared of its mound of papers hastily, and took his usual seat on a sagging Chesterfield.

"Shall I be mother?" she said coyly, fluttering her eyelashes at him.

Harold almost blushed like a schoolboy, "Indeed, madam, thank you kindly."

As she poured the tea and added the five sugar cubes which he requested, Harold thought he detected a small tremor in the lady's hands. Assuming it was a nervous anticipation for what was surely about to pass between them, Harold bestowed upon her his most gracious smile, which some rather ungrateful females had in the past told him more resembled a leer. Accepting the cup and saucer gratefully, and the proffered scone, Harold settled back into his chair.

"So, my dear, what brings you up here?"

Instead of answering, the woman simply looked on as Harold's hand reached to his mouth and he took a huge bite of the baked treat.

"You do," she whispered, as Harold felt his breath begin to shorten, his chest to tighten, his tongue to swell and his throat to close.

The dropped plate smashed on the parquet floor, as Harold grasped his throat and managed to gargle, "What the..?" He staggered towards his guest, who simply moved out of his range.

"Peanut," she spoke clearly and with a sadistic smile, as Harold noticed for the first time the smudge of bright red lipstick on the woman's teeth, as if it had been applied by someone unused to doing so. It made her look like one of those clowns in a horror film. Why he would notice that, of all things now, Harold wondered as he collapsed to the floor, his body convulsing.

The last things he saw were her stilettoed feet stepping over him as the woman went to retrieve the rest of the scones, and the china cups and saucers for washing. She reached down to check Harold's pulse, giving a nod of approval as she found none, before quickly collecting up the fallen remnants along with the broken pieces of crockery, and leaving the room silently.

Nought could be heard but the ticking of the antique Grandfather clock in the corner and the squawk of the parrot, shouting "Peanut" on repeat.

Ten Months Later

Flora looked around her at the six small tables, all set out with fine china cups and saucers in co-ordinating colours, lace doilies, floral tablecloths and silver cutlery. She smiled to herself, content in all she had achieved since coming to Baker's Rise a few months ago. The tearoom in the old stables, closed up for several years, had been given a new lease of life with a fresh lick of paint and bunting hung around the rough walls. A new sign had been hung outside the door, advertising the 'Tearoom on The Rise' – Flora liked to keep things simple and elegant. She ran her hands down her smart apron and patted her hair to ensure she was as smart as possible, before checking her watch for the fifth time in as many minutes. Still half an hour remained till opening time. The local baker, George Jones, had dropped off the day's delicacies an hour ago, and Flora had already arranged them in the display cabinet and fridge. Scones with clotted cream from the local farm and jam from the farm shop, teacakes, iced buns, custard tarts… a whole list of tempting treats for what Flora hoped would be her many customers, keen to try out the new tearoom on opening day. Flora wished to be baking some of the goods herself before too long, once she'd found someone in the village to teach her. She would start out as easily as possible, she had decided, and try to perfect the traditional English scone.

Flora had advertised the tearoom's opening in the local parish newsletter, the aptly titled, "What's on the Rise in Baker's Rise," as well as on the church notice board. She had tried to spread the news by word of mouth too, though this was more difficult as Flora was new to the village. She had quickly realised that folk here were not too keen on newcomers. Trust had to be earned, and civility only turned to friendship when you had embedded yourself suitably in village life. Flora hoped desperately that this would be a quicker process for her than for most, since she wished the tearoom to become a hub of village life. Mindful that any customers would have to travel halfway up the small hill, The Rise, to reach her, she had already thought about special offers and loyalty schemes to tempt people her way. Probably getting ahead of herself, Flora knew, but after coming from a fast-paced and highly structured job in the city, she was already struggling to fill her days and occupy her quick mind.

The bell on the door chimed and Flora was shocked from her musings. It was still too early for customers.

"Flora? Are you here?" The polished tone of the local solicitor, Harry Bentley, put Flora at her ease as she rushed from behind the counter to greet him. His grey hair popped around the door which he had only opened a fraction, followed by his wide-rimmed spectacles and his red, bulbous nose.

"Harry! What a lovely surprise!" the elderly gent, who should have been long since retired by now but still took an interest in the affairs of the village residents, had been Flora's sole friend and confidant since she'd arrived. It was he who had originally contacted her about the estate, he who had advised she should keep her true identity a secret until she had been accepted by the villagers. Harry had arranged the refurbishment of the coach house for Flora per her instructions from London, and had suggested the tearoom as a viable business opportunity. He had met her when she arrived and had visited her several times since, always with a friendly smile and a word of advice.

"Just thought I'd come to wish you luck on your first day, dear! Well, doesn't it look splendid! Very pretty indeed."

"Oh thank you, Harry, it wouldn't be anything without your recommendations and advice. Thank you for suggesting the farm shop, by the way, the jam and honey is delicious!"

"Not at all, my dear, now where are we with all the paperwork up at the big house?"

"Well, as you know there is mounds of it, I have only been able to shift the tip of the iceberg really. I know, it's my own fault. Being an actuary for so many years, I can't throw a single sheet of paper away without first reading what's on it! It makes the process slow and laborious, but I'm not in a hurry. The whole place is becoming dilapidated anyway. As you know, I've used the funds I could get my hands on to do up the coach house and this stable block. I'll have to wait to receive my divorce settlement before I can begin anything else. Hopefully, the villagers will have accepted me by then and it won't need to be so cloak and dagger," she gave a rueful smile and offered Harry a coffee from the new machine, which Flora had only just begun to learn how to use.

Eyeing the large silver monstrosity with distrust, Harry opted for a cup of tea, and sat down at the table nearest the counter.

"Aye, you've accomplished a lot in a few months, slow and steady wins the race especially in a place like Baker's Rise!"

"Indeed," Flora joined him at the table, a pot of tea for two and two toasted teacakes set in front of them. They chatted happily, until Flora looked at her watch and realised she should have changed the small sign on the door to 'open' some fifteen minutes ago. Not that she need worry, it was hardly as if she had a queue of customers waiting outside.

"I'll go and leave you to it. Remember to phone me if you need anything. On my home phone, mind, I still haven't worked out this mobile thing that my nephew gave me."

"Thank you, Harry," Flora busied herself clearing the table as she heard Harry's old BMW driving away on the gravel driveway. She took a deep breath, closed her eyes, and prayed that luck would be on her side and bring her some customers on her first day.

ABOUT THE AUTHOR

Rachel Hutchins lives in northeast England with her husband, three children and their dog Boudicca. She loves writing both mysteries and romances, and enjoys reading these genres too. Her favourite place is walking along the local coastline, with a coffee and some cake!

You can connect with Rachel and sign up to her quarterly **newsletter** via her website at: www.authorrachelhutchins.com

Alternatively, she has social media pages on:

Facebook: www.facebook.com/rahutchinsauthor

Instagram: www.instagram.com/ra_hutchins_author

OTHER MYSTERY BOOKS BY R. A. HUTCHINS

Here Today, Scone Tomorrow

Baker's Rise Mysteries Book One

When the self-titled Lord of the Manor, Harold Baker, meets an untimely end, the residents of Baker's Rise believe that he has simply died from choking. It is fair to say that they are certainly not sad to see him go!

Former city dweller Flora Miller, new to the quaint English village and in charge of the recently restored Tearoom on the Rise, is the unlucky recipient of the late man's parrot. Her new feathered companion has no filter and a vibrant personality that cannot be ignored! Witness to Harold's murder, the bird won't let the matter lie, and it's not long before Flora becomes suspicious.

A quest to bake the perfect scone is put on hold whilst Flora helps the charming Detective Bramble to investigate Harold's death. She has set her hopes on writing the next bestseller, not on becoming an amateur sleuth, but life sometimes has surprises in store!

Will they find the killer before they strike again, and can Flora find the acceptance and friendship she seeks amongst her new neighbours?

Packed with twists and turns, colourful characters and a sprinkle of romance, this is the first book in the series of Baker's Rise Mysteries. It will certainly leave you hungry for more!

(Includes a traditional scone recipe!)

There are currently ten books available in this series.

ROMANCES BY THIS AUTHOR

The Angel and the Wolf

What do a beautiful recluse, a well-trained husky, and a middle-aged biker have in common?
Find out in this poignant story of love and hope!

When Isaac meets the Angel and her Wolf, he's unsure whether he's in Hell or Heaven.
Worse still, he can't remember taking that final step.
They say that calm follows the storm, but will that be the case for Isaac?

Fate has led him to her door,
Will she have the courage to let him in?

To Catch A Feather

Found in Fife Book One

When tragedy strikes an already vulnerable Kate Winters, she retreats into herself, broken and beaten. Existing rather than living, she makes a journey North to try to find herself, or maybe just looking for some sort of closure.

Cameron McAllister has known his own share of grief and love lost. His son, Josh, is now his only priority. In his forties and running a small coffee shop in a tiny Scottish fishing village, Cal knows he is unlikely to find love again.

When the two meet and sparks fly, can they overcome their past losses and move on towards a shared future, or are the memories which haunt them still too real?

These books, as well as others by Rachel, can be found on Amazon worldwide in e-book and paperback formats, as well as free to read on Kindle Unlimited.

Printed in Great Britain
by Amazon

28923071R00106